# The Apple

D1103648

Also by Michel Faber

*Some Rain Must Fall and Other Stories*
*Under the Skin*
*The Hundred and Ninety-Nine Steps*
*The Courage Consort*
*The Crimson Petal and the White*
*The Fahrenheit Twins*

# MICHEL FABER

# *The* APPLE

### NEW
### *CRIMSON PETAL*
### STORIES

**CANONGATE**

*Edinburgh · New York · Melbourne*

The Text Publishing Company
Swann House
22 William St
Melbourne Victoria 3000
Australia
www.textpublishing.com.au
www.canongate.net

A Canongate Book published by The Text Publishing Company 2006

Designed by James Hutcheson
Typeset in Van Dijck by Palimpsest Book Production Ltd, Stirlingshire
Printed and bound by Griffin Press

ISBN 1 921145 62 5.
ISBN-13 978 1 921145 62 9.

'Christmas in Silver Street' was written in December 2002 and first published in Glasgow's *Sunday Herald*.

'Chocolate Hearts from the New World' was written in January 2003 and first issued as a limited-edition chapbook by Harcourt Brace.

The other stories were written in 2005.

My thanks, as always, to Eva.

# CONTENTS

# Foreword

Some people never read forewords, or read them only after they've finished the book, in case the introduction spoils the story. Other people value suspense so little, or fear nasty surprises so much, that they flip straight to the last page of a book and check how it ends. I can only presume that very few readers of my novel *The Crimson Petal and the White* flipped straight to the final page, because so many of them let me know how bereft they felt when they got there.

*The Crimson Petal* was, and is, an 835-page tale set in 1870s London. It follows the progress of a young woman called Sugar, a prostitute who longs to escape the influence of her abusive mother. By the end of the book, she is working as a nanny and has formed a close bond with a little girl called Sophie. There is every reason to hope that Sugar, damaged though she undoubtedly is by her past, will not perpetuate the cycle of abuse. But hope is not the same thing as knowing for sure. At the very end, Sugar and

Sophie are forced onto the streets. What happens next is undisclosed.

A few days ago, I lugged out the cardboard box where I keep letters from my readers. I re-read the ones about *The Crimson Petal*. Most of them were wonderfully generous and enthusiastic; several of them were from people who'd been readers for decades and had never written to an author before.

Here are some of the things I found:

Ever since I was a child in Cape Bruton, Nova Scotia, I have loved to read. There are some books which illuminate why that is, and remind a person how thankful we should be for those who write. *The Crimson Petal and the White* moved me so deeply, and taught me so much, in the process of a wonderful escape into another time . . . I wish I could articulate more lucidly all that your work made me think about and feel. Thank you for your gift.

This lady was unusual in not demanding to be told what happened after the ending of the novel. Most people who wrote to me were not so serene. Quite a few described themselves as 'in shock' or 'desperate'. A lady in New York began her letter:

> How dare you, sir? What an ending!

A man in Arnhem, The Netherlands, anticipated my position as he made his pitch:

> It is very clear why the story ends where it ends. You have made your point . . . Still I would like to request a sequel, for the following reasons:
>
> I have grown attached to Sugar, your and my heroine. In my own real life there have been a number of sudden and irrevocable goodbyes, which have left lasting feelings of pain and guilt. Why do you make me suffer more?

Another man assured me that:

> I could easily have read another 800 pages. So I implore you to please, please, *please*, PLEASE continue the story in a sequel.

Another man – the author of a tough, gritty contemporary Scottish novel – showed a touching concern for little Sophie:

About the ending; you are writing a sequel, aren't you? Sophie grows up to be a woman-before-her-time, maybe an author herself?

Another young man, from Texas — also, by remarkable coincidence, a published novelist — showed considerable ambivalence towards my book:

> *The Crimson Petal and the White* is singularly the most frustrating, maddening masterwork that I have ever trudged through in my entire life . . . How dare your book end with us not knowing what happened to Agnes! And where did Sugar take Sophie off to anyhow? Novels aren't supposed to just stop! Novels aren't like real life. Novels are supposed to have satisfying tight endings.

More conciliatory was the lady from Bournemouth, Dorset, speaking on behalf of a group of 'avid readers of mature years'. Her postcard, decorated with pussycats, read:

> Thank you so much. However, where did Sugar and Sophie go? Australia? New Zealand? Back

north? Please — if *you* know — give us an idea.
We worry about Sophie!!

A 65-year-old woman from Quebec was given the
book as a Christmas present and initially had her
doubts:

> I had never heard of you and, at 835 pages, I
> wondered if I would ever have the courage, and
> the *physical* strength to hold the book on my
> lap! I took it home and read the first line. That's
> all it took . . . Just before I end this letter, please
> tell me: where did Sugar go????? Did she indeed
> bring the child back to her mother???? What
> happens to them? You must write a sequel.

A woman from Aurora, Colorado confessed that she
had not slept for two days and called in sick for work
in order to read the novel in one marathon session:

> I simply won't be able to sleep until I've sent
> this off. About five minutes ago I finished your
> work *The Crimson Petal and the White*. I would
> have been writing this five minutes earlier but
> I was too stunned by your ending . . .

A lady in Michigan tackled the book in a slightly more leisurely mode:

> I've spent two weeks entranced by *The Crimson Petal and the White* with only a few breaks for meals and an occasional tennis or bridge game. And I didn't think I liked historical novels. After finishing at 1 a.m., I spent the rest of the night wondering what happened to Sugar, Agnes and William, the cad. You can't leave me hanging; please issue a news bulletin regarding their fates.

A corporate lawyer wrote:

> I wonder if you can resolve a dispute as to the interpretation of the ending of your book. I am a member of an all-male book group . . . Everybody but me thought the ending meant that Sugar took Sophie to meet Agnes and they all lived happily ever after.

I was touched by the goodwill of a man from New York City:

I just now – this second – said goodbye, knowing that it must be so. All week I had to pinch myself as a reminder that my new friends were not forever – but until the end of the week or maybe a little longer. Now they are gone – I hope to greater heights.

Particularly haunting was this hand-written note from a gentleman in Lancashire:

A few days before Christmas I was half awake and the first thought that came to me was what I could obtain as Christmas presents for Miss Sophie, Sugar and Mrs Fox. Then suddenly I realised who they really were.

There were many other people who communicated with me. Academics, women on welfare, historians, campaigners for social justice. I even corresponded with several prostitutes who announced that they *were* Sugar and had been spooked by my ability to spy on their thoughts as they were dealing with customers. All in all, my novel had made a powerful impression on an extraordinary range of people. I didn't send replies to as many as I would have liked, because I grew tired of explaining that there was not going to be a sequel. Sugar has been denied privacy all her life, I would say, and by the end of the novel she has earned the right to make her own way in the world, unscrutinised by us. And isn't it fun, at the end of a book, to be challenged to do what the Victorians were obliged to do between instalments of serialised novels: construct what happens next in our imaginations? In any case, the ending of *The Crimson Petal* is not as sudden as it might first appear. Re-read the final chapters, and you will find that there is a gradual process of leave-taking, a drawing of curtains, a succession of narrative farewells to each of the key characters. Yes, their future is uncertain. But so are all our futures. Only death concludes the story, and Sugar and Sophie are still alive. A sequel would crush that life out of them.

So, here I am in 2006, presenting a collection of *Crimson Petal* stories. Have I changed my mind about sequels?

No. This is a book of stories about characters who also appeared in *The Crimson Petal and the White*. You needn't have read that book in order to appreciate this one. The stories are, as stories should be, little worlds of their own.

They are also a much more wide-ranging time-travel experience than *The Crimson Petal* was. Some of the characters in these new stories are very much younger than they were in the novel, some are very much older. One tale is a memoir of the Edwardian era, narrated in the 1990s by the son of one of *Petal*'s characters – a reminder of how few human lifespans it takes to link us to distant centuries. Yet the essential mysteries at the end of *The Crimson Petal* (What happened to Sugar? Where did she and Sophie go?) are left intact.

Inevitably, though, the three stories that are set after the end of *Petal* – 'Clara and the Rat Man', 'Medicine' and 'A Mighty Horde Of Women In Very Big Hats, Advancing' – offer glimpses of futures that may be different from the scenarios some readers imagined. For example, those folk who were convinced that Sugar must have been captured immediately after the end of the novel will have to concede that, as far as can be judged from these new tales, no such capture occurred. But we are still a very long way from knowing "what happened". These stories offer openings, not closure. Or, if they offer closure, it is of an instinctive, emotional kind.

None of which need concern readers who are

unfamiliar with these characters' history. The tales collected here are complete narratives, and if *The Crimson Petal* had never existed, I would wish to have written them regardless. 'A Mighty Horde . . .' gives me as much satisfaction as my best novels. In fact, to my mind, it *is* a novel, with a novel's scope and richness of theme. It's done with fewer words, that's all.

But why these characters, and not others? Why this slim volume, and not more? Because these were the tales that demanded to exist. There were other characters I was curious about, characters I wished I could spend more time with. They had moved away, disappeared into history. I had to let them go. My one serious regret is that I didn't manage to write a story about Henry Rackham, a decent man who deserved so much more than he got in *The Crimson Petal*. I offered him an opportunity to live again, as a younger person, even as a child; I urged him to seize the chance to say the things he'd been too shy to say the first time round. He remained too shy.

Such things must be respected.

This, then, is all there is. I can understand why some readers might still wish to know more about what

became of Sugar. Revisiting my accumulated correspondence, I wish I knew what became of some of the
readers who took the trouble to write to me. The man
who had cancer and read *The Crimson Petal* in hospital:
is he still alive? The prostitute who said she was leaving
the game and returning to education: did she? And so
on. But I will probably never know.

But then, I'd thought I would never know the
things in these stories. And now I know.

Michel Faber, 2006

Christmas in Silver Street

lose your eyes. Lose track of time for a moment – just long enough to be overtaken by a hundred and thirty years. It's December 1872. Feathery snow is falling on that dubious part of London between Regent Street and Soho, a hodge-podge of shops and houses crammed between the opulent avenues of the well-to-do and the festering warrens of the poor. Welcome to Silver Street. Here umbrella-makers, scriveners, piano tuners, unsuccessful playwrights, dressmakers and prostitutes live side by side, each pursuing their trade under worsening weather. Snow makes everyone and everything look equal, as if God has lovingly applied a thin layer of white icing to rooftops, street-stalls, carriages, and the heads of beggars. Suffering and decrepitude are scarcely recognisable under such a pretty disguise.

On this frigid December morning, you have entered a brothel known as Mrs Castaway's, and are peeking into an upstairs bedroom. What have you found? A girl called Sugar. She's seventeen, and you are watching her inspect her tongue in a hand-mirror.

Do you know Sugar? If you are a man, there is a good chance you have known her in the Biblical sense. She's a prostitute, and at this point in Queen Victoria's reign the ratio of prostitutes to the overall population is 1:36, or one per twelve adult males.

If you are a respectable woman, you ought to pretend you never heard such statistics, and ought to hurry past Sugar in the street, fearful of suffering a stain on your reputation. But perhaps you are not as respectable as all that, for you have not passed by. You are here, watching Sugar inspect her tongue in a brothel.

Do not be scandalised by Sugar's age. The age of consent for girls is twelve. In two years from now, it will be raised to thirteen. Sugar is an old hand at this game.

She sits in her rumpled bed, holding the mirror to her face. Her tongue, she notes, is grey in the middle, not bright pink the way it ought to be. She drank too much last night, and here is the evidence.

Last night was Christmas Eve, now it's the morning after. December 25th, a day like any other. Sugar has the lamps lit, because her bedroom window is small and the sun is lost behind the grey swirl of snow. The fireplace spits and hisses; the floorboards creak by themselves. The old-fashioned erotic prints on the walls are, as ever, the only decorations; Mrs Castaway does not encourage her girls to deck their halls with boughs of holly.

To be frank, none of the shabby Georgian houses jumbled behind Silver Street is the best place to see evidence of Yuletide festivities; for that, you would need to go to the West End, or the suburbs. Only in the splendour of the Burlington Arcade can there be a wholesale celebration of gift-giving; only in the villas of the respectable can fairytales of Virgin Birth survive.

Sugar takes one last look at the inside of her mouth. How odd, she thinks, that red wine can turn a pink tongue grey. The miracle of the body's perversity.

A knock at her door makes her jump. At this time of the morning, she knows it can't be a customer. It must be little Christopher, come to collect the bed-linen.

'I'm 'ere for the sheets,' says the boy, when she opens the door to him. He's blond, blue-eyed and as innocent-looking as a shepherd's lad from a Nativity scene. Not exactly dressed in rags, although his shirt and trousers would benefit from some mending here and there. Amy, his mother, is not the mending type. Her speciality is thrashing grown-up men until they whimper for mercy.

How old is little Christopher? Sugar can't tell. Far too young to be a drudge in a brothel, but Amy has put him to work this way, and he seems grateful to have a purpose. Perhaps if he washes and dries a million bed-sheets, he will finally make amends for his original sin – of being born.

'Thank you, Christopher,' says Sugar.

He doesn't reply, merely begins folding the dirty sheets into a stack he can carry away. Outside in the street, a fruity voice begins to sing:

*On the first day of Christmas, my true love gave to me*
*A partridge in a pear tree . . .*

'It's Christmas, then,' says the boy, lifting the pile of linen to his chest.

'Yes, Christopher.'

He nods, as if confirming something he knows inside out, something he mentioned only for conversation's sake. Chin resting on a wad of soiled linen, he walks to the door and is about to leave, then turns and asks,

'What's Christmas?'

Sugar blinks, momentarily stumped. 'It's the day Jesus Christ was born,' she replies.

'I knowed that,' says the boy.

From outside: '*Four collie birds, three French hens, two turtle doves, and a partridge in a pear tree . . .*'

'He was born in a manger,' adds Sugar, to make the story more interesting for him. 'A big wooden tub for animals to eat from.'

Christopher nods. Making-do and poverty is the way of the world, he knows.

'*. . . my true love gave to me, five gold rings . . .*'

'Some folk,' observes the boy, 'gives presents at Christmas. To each uvver, like.'

'So they do, Christopher.'

The child shakes his head, like a little old man bemused by the pointlessness of giving someone six-pence in exchange for sixpence. He hugs the bed-sheets tight to his chest and walks out of the room, craning his head sideways to make sure he doesn't break his neck on the stairs.

'*Six geese a-laying,*' carols the voice from the streets outside, '*five gold rings, four collie birds, three French hens . . .*'

Sugar shuts her bedroom door; there's a draught

getting in. She throws herself back onto the half-stripped bed, irritable, wishing the day was over instead of scarcely begun. The pillow-cases smell of men's hair-oil and spirits; she ought to have sent them downstairs with the rest of the washing.

The carol-singer loitering in the street outside Mrs Castaway's seems indefatigable. Snow continues to whirl through the sky, the windowpanes rattle and creak, but still those damned partridges and turtle-doves proliferate. Passersby must be tossing coins to this bawling nuisance; better they should throw stones.

After a few more minutes, Sugar can stand it no longer. She leaps up and gets properly dressed, putting on stays, fresh warm stockings, a demure black-and-grey striped dress with a quilted bodice, a smart purple jacket. She brushes her hair and winds it into a tight chignon, then pins a charcoal-and-purple bonnet to her scalp. She might be a fashionable widow in half-mourning.

By the time Sugar leaves Mrs Castaway's and steps onto the snowy cobblestones of Silver Street, the snow has stopped falling, and the carol-singer has melted away.

★  ★  ★

Not all the shops are open, Sugar finds. A worrying trend. Are we heading for a future when everything shuts at Christmas? God forbid.

Still, there are enough establishments open for her purposes. The stationer's has a full display of Christmas cards in the window, garlanded with tinsel, cotton-wool snow and robins made of fabric remnants. After long deliberation, Sugar chooses a card that performs an amusing trick when a paper tag is pulled — an angel whose wings flap. Such clever things they make nowadays; there seems no end to the ingenuity of modern manufacture.

In a confectioner's a few doors along, she seriously considers buying a prettily packaged box of chocolates, but fears the assortment will not be to her taste. Instead, she bids the shopkeeper fill a paper bag with dark chocolate pralines, her favourites.

The poulterer's shop is slightly disappointing by comparison. All the fine, plump birds which she recalls hanging there only a few days ago — chickens with rosettes pinned to their breasts, huge turkeys with comically dangling heads, clutches of ducklings — are gone now, gobbled up by the ovens of the prosperous. At this moment they're no doubt filling the busy kitchens of respectable houses with the smell of roast meat and savoury stuffing. Here in the poulterer's shop on Christmas afternoon, only a few scraggy birds remain. Sugar chooses the best of them, a chicken.

In the street, tempting the impetuous and the dirt-poor, hawkers are selling toys and trifles for children – balloons, paper windmills, mice made of sweet dough. Sugar buys several mice from a leering old man, bites the head off one, chews thoughtfully, spits it out.

With every step of her superior black boots, Sugar ventures deeper into the network of poorer streets hidden behind the thoroughfare. From a greengrocer's barrow she buys a few carrots and pota-toes, and walks on, swinging an increasingly heavy basket alongside her skirts. The farther she moves away from Regent Street, the more the opulence of the West End seems an absurd dream, punctured by the reality of squalor.

At last she finds a bakery whose stock-in-trade is not fancy cakes and pastries, but copious amounts of cheap bread. Its clientele is the poor wretches who live in the crumbling lodging-houses and hovels all about here. A queue of customers – ragamuffins, street vendors, Irishwomen – jostles in the doorway and spills out into the street; this baker not only bakes bread but cooks entire dinners for families who don't possess an oven. Hours of roasting can be bought for a pittance, and, for an additional halfpenny, a generous ladleful of the baker's own special gravy is thrown into the bargain.

Sugar waits for ninety minutes near the baker's. She could have gone home and waited there, but waiting on the street is something she is good at. She takes refuge for a while inside a chandler's, pretending to be interested in buying some stolen goods. When her toes have defrosted and the chandler is beginning to annoy her, she moves on. Three passersby offer to rent her affections; she refuses.

At the appointed time she returns for her Christmas meal. The baker greets her with a dis-tracted smile; his brown beard is powdered white with flour. Ah, yes, the lassie with the chicken, he remembers now.

The dishes and bowls into which the piping-hot food has been transferred are chipped and stained, barely fit for a drunkard's street-stall, but even so, the baker obliges Sugar to pay him a shilling, as a security in case she fails to return them. He can tell she's never done this before; other customers bring their own pots and crockery.

'Mind you come back tomorrow,' he warns. Sugar nods, though she hasn't the least intention of returning this miserable bric-a-brac. She can earn a shilling in ten minutes of lying on her bed.

'Merry Christmas,' she winks, as she balances her heavy-laden basket in the crook of her arm.

By the time Sugar has walked back to Mrs Castaway's, the food has lost a good deal of its heat. This hiring of ovens is, after all, a service designed for labourers' families waiting hungrily around the corner from the baker's, not for prostitutes in Silver Street. Moreover, by the time Sugar has located Christopher and summoned him up to her bedroom, and the basket's contents are finally unveiled to the astonished boy, the chicken is barely lukewarm. Nevertheless it releases a delicious smell, and the roast vegetables twinkle in their juicy dishes. It may not be a feast borne by servants in a halo of steam, but by the standards of Mrs Castaway's on a snowy afternoon, it's an exotic surprise.

Sugar carves a hunk off the chicken's breast, another off the drumstick, and doles these onto a fresh plate along with some potato and carrot. She adds a big spoonful of the baker's special stuffing, scrapes some gravy from the bottom of the dish.

'Here,' she says evenly, handing the plate to Christopher. 'Merry Christmas.'

The boy's face is inscrutable as he takes the food from her; he might almost be accepting a pile of washing. Nevertheless, he sits on a footstool and balances the plate on his knees. With his fingers, he begins to transfer the food to his mouth.

Sugar eats with him. There's a vaguely muttony taste to the chicken, suggesting that two very different animals sat side by side during their sojourn in the communal oven. Even so, it's good.

'I should've bought something to drink,' she mutters. Next to the bed, there's half a bottle of red wine left over from last night; too potent for a child who's accustomed to diluted beer.

'I don't need nuffink,' says Christopher, popping another roast potato into his mouth.

'Here's a card, too,' says Sugar, and produces it. Observing that his fingers are otherwise occupied and greasy, she demonstrates the action of the paper angel's wings by pulling on the tab. Christopher smiles broadly. She can't recall ever seeing him smile before.

Outside in the street, a tuneless female voice

begins to sing. It's not 'The Twelve Days of Christmas' this time, nor even a festive song. Instead, this worthy woman, employing her considerable lungpower in the attempt to penetrate the walls and windows of Mrs Castaway's, bawls:

> *For you upon this blessed morn,*
> *Of Virgin Mother undefiled,*
> *An Infant all Divine is born,*
> *And God becomes a little Child.*

Christopher's smile broadens. He is almost unrecognisable, with deep creases in his cheeks, a twinkle in his eye, and a dark grease-smudge on his nose.

'Have a sip of wine,' says Sugar, handing him the bottle. 'Not too much, though; it will turn your tongue grey.'

Christopher takes a swig from the bottle. Do not be scandalised: he's had strong drink all his life, and wine is cleaner than water.

> *No palace hath He but a shed,*
> *No cradle but a manger mean:*
> *Yet o'er that peerless Infant's Head*
> *A new and wondrous star is seen . . .*

'Here, have a mouse,' says Sugar, setting one of the sweet dough fancies on the floor in front of him. 'They're not very good. Scarcely fit for mice to eat.'

Christopher, having scoffed his Christmas meal, takes a cautious nibble at the confectionery.

'Nuffink wrong wiv it,' he pronounces, and bites the creature in half.

Sugar is relieved he likes it; she'd meant to give him some chocolates, but her own greed got the better of her, and she ate them all while waiting for the meal to be cooked. There is a limit to human generosity, even at Christmas.

'That's me finished,' says Christopher suddenly. 'Give me them pillercases.'

Sugar stares at him uncomprehending for a moment, then removes the pillow-slips from her pillows and hands them to the boy.

'Forgot,' he remarks. It's not clear which of them he is blaming for the oversight.

Somewhat awkwardly, he walks to the door, hesitates, then ducks back to claim his angel card with the moving wings.

'I'll bring it back,' he assures her.

Sugar yearns to tell him there is no need, it's his, and that he should've had chocolates if she weren't such a greedy, hard-hearted girl; that he should've had a pile of proper presents if his mother hadn't been Amy; that he should've had a decent home and a father and nice clothes and schooling if the world weren't such a pitiless and grubby place. She imagines herself embracing him, pressing him hard against her bosom, peppering his head with kisses – all the expressions of unfeigned affection she has read about in stories.

'No need,' she says hoarsely.

When Christopher has disappeared downstairs, Sugar lies back on her bed. The stripped pillows still smell of hair-oil and alcohol; only the passing of time will get rid of it. Outside, the evangelist has given up and moved on; thank God for small mercies. The snow has started again, tentatively, with the lightest possible flakes. All over London, these feathery wisps are settling on the rooftops of rich and poor alike, melting instantly where there is warmth, accumulating into a soft white blanket where there is none.

It is almost time to open your eyes; the twenty-first century is waiting for you, and you've been among prostitutes and strange children for too long. Come away now. Sugar is tired, even though it's the middle of the day. Tonight her work will begin anew, so where's the harm in taking a snooze while things are quiet? Half-asleep already, she leans in front of the looking-glass, wipes her face clean with a damp cloth, and sticks her tongue out.

Fancy that: her tongue is pink and healthy-looking. How quickly the human body recovers from its abuses! It's a miracle, hallelujah. Merry Christmas now, and sweet dreams.

Clara and the
Rat Man

lara had found the Rat Man repulsive from the outset, but, because she found *all* of her customers repulsive, this had seemed insufficient reason to spurn his advances. Looking back on it, she regretted her lack of discrimination, and blamed it on her inexperience as a prostitute. In the menagerie of maleness, two kinds of repulsive existed: repulsive-ugly and repulsive-peculiar. The Rat Man was repulsive-peculiar.

Not that he wasn't ugly, too. His teeth were brown, his eyes were bloodshot, his beard was wispy and his nose was pock-marked. He walked with a limp, and the pinkish-grey skin of his forehead was strangely scarred, as if someone had poured a kettle of scalding water onto his brow when he was a baby. Altogether he would have been a pitiable case, if Clara had been the pitying kind. The world was too undeserving, however, for Clara to give pity away for nothing. Ugly, scarred men were none the less men, and thus despicable.

'Call me Mr Heaton,' he'd said, with a formal bow. It was almost comical, him standing there in Great White Lion Street, leaning on his cane, treating her as though she were a prospective pupil of the pianoforte, rather than a whore.

That was six weeks ago. Six weeks was a long time in her new life. Once-cherished illusions and inhibitions were dying almost daily, and, just when she imagined that they must surely all have perished, a few more would fall. Each month, she was unrecognisable as the person she'd been the month before, and the month before that. Even her way of speaking sounded less well-educated, more common now than when she was a servant in a cosy middle-class house, as though the grime of street life had soiled her tongue, coarsening her vowels, nibbling the consonants away. The effort of refraining from saying 'ain't', or of avoiding double negatives, seemed too wearisome now that there was no-one to impress. Only twelve months backwards in time, dressed in stiff calico and clutching an impressive set of silvery keys, she had dealt with tradesmen and bakers' boys at the back door of her mistress's house, and had felt herself superior to them as soon as they opened their mouths. The smallest difference in intonation served to define her place above them on the ladder. But she had descended that ladder with dizzying speed.

Yet in another way, she was the stronger for her fall. Every day, she became more skilled and confident at taking the measure of a man in a single glance, and brushing him off if she suspected he was more trouble than he was worth. If the peculiar Mr Heaton had first accosted her yesterday instead of six weeks ago, she would have cold-shouldered him without hesitation. Yes, she was almost sure of that.

But a month and a half ago, she'd still been finding her feet in the profession, and fearful that her fastidious tastes might render her destitute. After all, she wasn't a fancy woman, kept in a smart house in St John's Wood. She was a common streetwalker, seeking to earn enough for lodgings and food. What would become of her if she said no to every ugly man who propositioned her?

Mr Heaton had not exactly propositioned her, in any case. He had merely asked her if, for a shilling, she would promise to let one of her fingernails grow.

'Fingernails grow awful slow, sir,' she'd said, once she'd got him to repeat the bizarre request. 'Do you want to stand 'ere watching while it 'appens?'

'No,' he'd replied. 'I'll meet you here next week

at the same time. If you've let the nail grow, I shall give you another shilling.'

It seemed absurdly easy money. He specified the nail she was to let grow (middle finger, right hand), she gave him her word, he gave her a shilling, and she watched him limp away. Morning turned to afternoon, afternoon turned to evening, and Clara's life went along its course. She spent the coin, forgot all about Mr Heaton. She forgot about him so thoroughly that she was loitering in the same spot the following week – and was mortified to see him approaching her once more.

She hoped that she might, by sheer coincidence, have neglected to trim the nail they'd agreed upon. But, when she removed her glove at Mr Heaton's request, the body part in question was down to the quick.

'I'm sorry, sir,' she said. 'I must've bit it.'

He looked melancholy, as if this identical circumstance had played itself out many times, with many other women.

'I'll give you another chance,' he said. 'And another shilling. But this time you must keep your promise.'

'I surely will, sir,' she'd pledged.

Her promise proved damned difficult to keep. Although her former life as a lady's maid was barely a year in the past, she seemed to have lost the knack of keeping in mind, during the routine activities of an average day, any responsibility that was not immediately obvious. Once upon a time, she'd been able to help her mistress plan a dinner party or sew a dress while not forgetting that at precisely five o'clock, she must remind her of some other thing. How extraordinary, to have been so disciplined! Nowadays, she could scarcely remember which services a customer had paid for, and often suspected that a man was helping himself to something extra.

As for this affair with the fingernail, it was torture. Ten, twenty times a day she would find the nail between her lips, just about to be gnawed off by her small white teeth. With a grunt of annoyance she would pull her hand away. Ten, twenty times a day, she would be vaguely, uneasily aware that one of her nails was ill-matched to the other nine, and wonder why. Oh yes: Mr Heaton.

Who would've thought that a slightly longer middle fingernail could be such a bother? It was nothing spectacular to look at, perhaps half an inch in extra length. Yet it caught on the fabric of her bodice, dug into the flesh of her neck when she was buttoning up her collar, scratched her cheek when she raised her hand to fiddle with the curls of her fringe. The normally snug fit of her glove was ruined. Half an inch of nail, and it might as well be a beastly talon!

After a day's work (Clara preferred to do her business during the day and sleep at night) she would retire to her room in Mrs Porter's lodging-house, and pay Mrs Porter's maid-of-all-work to fill a bath, and then she would soak in the warm water until her hands went soft and dimpled. And the nail would become pliable, so pliable she could bend it against the tip of her finger. If she were to put it between her teeth, she knew it would tear away without the least resistance, and would taste of nothing at all, and she could swallow it, or spit it out if she wished. She sucked the nail, took it between her teeth the way some men took her nipple, but left it intact. God damn Mr Heaton! How much longer would he plague her?

Each week he came to her at the corner of Great White Lion and Dudley Street, noted approvingly the growth of the nail, and gave her a shilling. Each week she resolved to tell him that she wanted no more shillings from him, that the length of her nail was too inconvenient. Each week she lost her nerve. Mr Heaton was so manifestly pleased with her for obeying him, and Clara couldn't help feeling a matchstick glow of childish pride at having met his expectations.

Men were not often pleased with Clara. She wasn't likeable or charming or even especially polite. She offered her body with bad grace, stated her prices matter-of-factly, didn't pretend to experience transports of joy when some red-faced fool was squirming against her. She scorned compliments; when one of her first customers told her she had the prettiest breasts he'd ever seen, she would probably have slapped him, had she not been attached to him at an awkward angle just then. The honeyed compliments of men always led to a slick of viscous liquid that would soil her clothing and need to be wiped away.

Mr Heaton, however, had not yet laid a hand on her. His shilling was by far the easiest earnings of her week; she got it in thirty seconds flat. Clara wondered if he was a eunuch. His limping gait, the scars on his face . . . perhaps these were signs of a more serious injury. Clara disliked sick animals and her instincts told her to keep well away from such things. But Jesus Christ almighty: a shilling in thirty seconds, without a hand laid on her! She couldn't justify rejecting such an offer, especially when other customers wasted hours of her time, haggled over prices, inflicted bruises on her flesh, made her itch. Each time she felt annoyed with Mr Heaton, she reminded herself that she'd had one, two, three, four, five, six shillings from him, for doing nothing. If she kept this lark up for twelve weeks, her accrued capital (ignoring for a moment that she spent each shilling as soon as she got it) would be a pound. A pound just for resisting the impulse to chew a fingernail! That couldn't be a bad thing, could it?

But then she discovered the catch. Last week, she'd found out something about her crippled benefactor that transformed him from 'Mr Heaton' into 'the Rat Man'.

They met in the street as usual. Passersby squinted in bemusement and distaste as she ungloved her right hand and allowed him to inspect her middle finger. Her nail was ever-so-slightly chipped, where she'd caught it on a brick wall while servicing a customer in a hurry, but it was long, and Mr Heaton nodded in satisfaction.

'Would you like to earn five shillings at a stroke?' he asked her, as she was tugging her glove back on.

She regarded him suspiciously. Was he going to ask her to allow four more of her nails to grow? This seemed the most obvious next proposal.

Instead, he said:

'I want you to accompany me to a sporting event.'

'I don't understand much about sport, sir,' she'd replied.

'That doesn't matter,' he assured her. 'Nobody would expect anything of you. All eyes will be on the action.'

'Yours too?'

'Mine too.'

'Then what use would I be to you, sir?'

He leaned in closer to her, closer than he'd ever ventured before. A respectable, fashionable mother, passing at that moment with her infant daughter toddling along beside, shielded the child's face and hurried her along the footpath, so shocking was this public display of intimacy. The sparse beard on Mr Heaton's chin almost brushed the shoulder of Clara's dress as he spoke low into her ear.

'The sporting event I have in mind is pit ratting. A publican of my acquaintance hosts a rat pit in Southwark on the last Thursday of every month. The next one is next week.'

'I don't like rats, sir.'

'You don't have to like rats. They come to a bad end, anyway, and swiftly. Dogs dispatch them with lightning speed.'

'I don't like dogs neither, sir.'

He winced, and his expression became somewhat supplicatory.

'Oh, don't say that. There will be two dogs there on Thursday. One of them is my own. Robbie is his name. He's the most beautiful dog; a handsomer dog never walked the earth. His coat is smoother than sable.'

'I won't have to do nothing with the dog, I hope, sir?'

'You can admire his skill. Or not, as you please. Your business will be with me.'

'And what business will that be, sir?'

'Nothing you won't have done before.'

'I was a respectable woman until this year, sir. There's many things I've never done.'

'Even so . . .' He inclined his head and smiled a weary smile, as if to imply that any whore worth a pinch of salt would have this particular trick in her repertoire.

An alarming thought entered Clara's head.

'I won't have to . . . *do it* with you in front of the other people in the public house, will I?'

'Of course not,' he said, in gruff exasperation. 'We will simply watch the rat-catching together. Fully clothed. The only thing I require of you is that you put your hand down the back of my trousers. No one will see it; I'll wear a long overcoat that will preserve us from prying eyes. Not that there are likely to be any on us. The rat pit is a source of great excitement. You have no idea how wound up people can get.'

Clara stared him straight in the face, which was her usual technique (now that she was a harlot of some experience) with untrustworthy customers. She focused on his pock-marked nose, trying not to be swayed by the feverish, imploring eyes on either side. She made an effort to riffle through his most recent utterances in reverse order, to retrieve the one that concerned her.

'Down the back of your trousers?' she said.

'Yes,' he said. 'When the . . . uh . . . performance is underway, you are to slip your hand into my clothing. I shan't be wearing anything under my trousers. You will insert your middle finger into my rectum.'

'Rectum, sir?'

'My arse-hole.'

'And then?'

'There is no "And then". That's all.' He paused. 'Five shillings.'

Clara stared at his forehead. It was shiny and seemed to be throbbing, as if the flesh was desperate to sweat but too badly scarred to do so.

'Blood makes me sick, sir.'

'There's scarcely any blood. It's not like dog-fights or cock-fights or bull-baiting. It's efficient. It's clean. It's . . .' He clenched his fists, frustrated by her lack of understanding. 'It's a privilege to behold it. Awe – that's what it inspires. Awe. It's a . . .' He took a deep breath; the normal amount of air was not sufficient to convey the grandeur. '. . . an amazing demonstration of what happens when a superbly trained creature is pitted against a horde of vermin.'

She had never heard him sound so passionate. She didn't care for it.

'The thing is, next Thursday is quite a full sort of day for me, sir.'

He grabbed her gloved hands, there in the street, and squeezed them inside his own. His eyes were luminous with sincerity.

'Please,' he said. 'I've given you a shilling a week,

just to prepare for this. Don't deny me. Everything depends on you. You'll be finished in an hour.'

'You frighten me, sir.'

'Ten shillings, then.'

Clara swallowed hard.

'All right,' she said.

Since then, Clara had put a great deal of thought into how she might renege on her promise without suffering unpleasant consequences.

She considered spending Thursday entirely indoors, ironing her clothes, mending the seam in her camisole, and generally giving her body a rest. But there was no telling what the Rat Man might do if frustrated in this fashion. He might look for her every day afterwards.

She considered brazening it out, telling him she'd had second thoughts, and showing him a middle finger neatly clipped. If he got angry, she could simply call for assistance, couldn't she? London was crawling with policemen lately, as well as do-gooders of all kinds. Surely one of them would come to her rescue? 'This man is making indecent propositions to me,' she could plead. But perhaps this was not a very wise idea after all. She was known by sight to several local policemen.

If there was a complaint against her from a gentleman (however ugly or scarred he might be), they would cheerfully throw her in prison.

She considered murdering the Rat Man, just to remove him from her life. But she had to admit that this seemed an excessive response to her fear of embarrassment, more the sort of response one might expect from a man than a woman. Also, she had no means of killing anyone, not even a knife. Was she supposed to strangle Mr Heaton in the street? The whole notion was daft, and she didn't know why she'd even thought of it, other than the thrill it offered.

She considered fleeing altogether, plying her trade in a different part of the city. Lord Jesus, one little nail grown half an inch, and here she was, planning to wrench herself away from St Giles just as she was getting the hang of it! But this, too, was mere fantasy. Her preferred lodgings were with Mrs Porter in Queen Street and there was a nice public house near the Broad Street junction where she had a growing reputation as a clean girl with not a mark on her. Also there was Dickie's Chophouse in Seven Dials, where she could eat as much as she wanted, within reason, as long as she never spoke a word to Mr Dickie's wife.

No, she must keep her appointment with the Rat Man.

Thursday came, and Clara rendezvoused with Mr Heaton in the usual place. Without further discussion, she fell into step with him as he limped briskly along Dudley Street. He was dressed in a voluminous, knee-length overcoat which made him look like an impresario. A down-at-heel impresario, perhaps: the coat was slightly moth-eaten. For the first time it occurred to Clara that her benefactor might not be especially wealthy. Could he ill afford the money he'd been giving her? She felt a twinge of conscience, and dealt with it the only way she knew.

'I want my ten shillings now,' she said.

He handed them to her even as they walked. As if he'd been expecting this moment and had the coins already enclosed in his palm.

How would they get to Southwark, she wondered? It must be quite far from here, as none of her prostitute friends knew of it. Did the Rat Man mean to take her on an exhausting march, or would they board an omnibus together, like husband and wife? She didn't like the idea of hordes of strangers presuming that there must be an intimate relationship between herself and the Rat Man; she wished she'd fobbed him off with a simple fuck six weeks ago, instead of getting herself mixed up in this malarkey.

'Is it far?' she said.

His arm jerked into the air, and she flinched in fear of being struck, but he was only hailing a cab.

'The Traveller's Rest, Southwark,' he said.

'Very good, sir,' said the cabbie. 'Going for the *special keg* they keeps downstairs, are you sir?'

'Indeed.'

'I'm partial to a bit of that meself, sir. Very tasty.'

Clara and Mr Heaton climbed into the cabin. Mr Heaton seemed not at all surprised that the cabbie knew the reputation of The Traveller's Rest. For a moment, Clara caught a glimpse of a London which was vastly richer in attractions than she and her cronies had any notion of, and which other folk made it their business to explore. It was not a picture she had any desire to see. Indeed, the Rat Man seemed to be specialise in showing her glimpses of things she would prefer to remain ignorant of.

'How will I get home when it's over?'

The Rat Man smiled sadly. 'I trust we'll both agree when it's over.'

'But you don't live where I live.'

'I'll take you home first.'

Clara nodded, unconvinced. If she'd learned anything since her fall into prostitution, it was not to
rely on the courtesy and generosity of others. The
cab seemed to be travelling a very long way, and every
clack of the horse's hooves on the cobbles emphasised
that she was farther and farther from the streets she
knew. The ten shillings stowed in the pocket of her
dress would do her no good if she was robbed and left
for dead in a dark unfamiliar neighbourhood. To prevent that happening, she was now under pressure to
remain on good terms with the Rat Man, to please
him or at least not quarrel with him. She didn't know
if it was possible for them to spend a whole afternoon
together, especially one involving rats and dogs,
without quarrelling.

'I hope we have understood each other about the
nail,' he said, his face turned away from her in the
shadowy cabin.

'The nail, sir?'

'You mustn't be gentle with it, you understand?
You must push it as deep inside as your finger will
go.'

'I'll do me best, sir.'

'You needn't worry about hurting me.'

'I won't, sir.'

'And don't pull it out until . . .' He turned even more sharply away from her, as though he had just spotted someone of his acquaintance passing by in the street. 'Until it's over.'

'How can I be sure of that, sir?'

He turned to face her then. His mouth was set hard. The scarred flesh on his face was pale, while his cheeks were flushed and mottled.

'The last rat will be dead,' he said.

The Traveller's Rest was on the other side of the world. The cab had to cross the Thames to get there, past Waterloo, where Clara had been once or twice with her mistress, and then farther still. The pub itself, when they finally reached it, hardly seemed to warrant the length of the journey. It impressed Clara as a low sort of establishment, the kind where shiftless men drank with serious intent. The atmosphere was brewed thick with pipe smoke and alcohol fumes, and the regulars hunched low as if to take the occasional breath of oxygen from somewhere under the tables. A patch of floor where the floorboards had rotted away was crudely mended with planks of a different colour, the jagged edges covered over with tar. The fireplace was choked with ash and amber embers. Several of the gaslights were turned off or had ceased to function, and the scarcity of glass in the room meant that it wholly lacked the mirrored conviviality of the pubs Clara frequented. Instead, dark brown wood stole the light and refused to give it back.

'I don't like it here,' she whispered to her companion.

'This isn't what we've come for,' he whispered back. 'What we've come for is downstairs.'

Clara couldn't see any stairs. She craned her head around a pillar, and saw only more half-sozzled men staring back at her from their drinking stations. She had expected a bright, theatrical-looking banner hung up to generate excitement about the impending rat fight, but there was nothing of the sort. Indeed there was scant decoration on the walls – just a few curling handbills advertising recently bygone entertainments in more salubrious-sounding establishments than The Traveller's Rest. There was also a hand-lettered notice saying 'BEWARE OF SODS'.

Mr Heaton walked up to the publican. They nodded at each other without a word, shook hands . . . or perhaps a coin was being passed from one man to the other. Then the publican, Mr Heaton and Clara passed through the room to the very rear, where the publican pulled open a trap-door in the floor. A flight of stairs was revealed, illuminated by a light of unclear origin. The tobacco vapours of the room below met those of the room above, and swirled into each other.

The cellar, when Clara had allowed herself to be led down the stairs, was really not such a dismal place. In fact, it suited her better. Despite its sub-terranean location, it seemed less claustrophobic than the drinking den upstairs, and was much better lit, with a dozen oil lamps at strategic points. The rough stone walls were painted white, to enhance the illumination.

The cellar was mainly given over to the rat pit. There were several rows of wooden seats pushed against the rough stone walls, but no-one was sit-ting in them. All the spectators – some twenty in all – stood around the edge of the pit, which was more like a raised wooden tub. It was octagonal, waist-high, and about nine feet in diameter. The pub-lican made his way over to a barrel almost as tall as himself, a barrel made for flour rather than wine or beer, to whose lid he laid his ear. Not quite satisfied, he peered into one of several holes drilled in the lid, squinting clownishly.

'Seventy-five of the best in there,' said a man wearing a top hat without any top on it.

'We could use a hundred,' said the publican.

'A nundred of these beauties takes more than one man to catch.'

'You used to catch a hundred for us.'

'That was before himprovements in sanitation.'

'Well, I hope these are big ones.'

'Big? Comb their fur a different way and they could pass as ferrets.'

Mr Heaton laid a finger against Clara's upper arm to get her attention.

'I'm going to fetch Robbie now,' he murmured near her ear. 'Things will move fast from here on in. Remember what I've asked of you.'

She nodded.

'Take your glove off, then,' he reminded her.

She looked down at her hands, self-conscious at the idea of removing her gloves in a public place: everyone would instantly assume she was a woman of low breeding. But then she realised she was the sole female in the cellar, and that each man must surely already have judged her to be a whore. She pulled off her gloves, finger by finger, and no-one took a blind bit of notice. She could have thrown her skirts over her head, and still the assembled spectators might have kept their attention squarely on the business at hand. Some of the men were already leaning their elbows on the rim of the rat-pit, jostling shoulder-to-shoulder. Clara wondered how it was decided who should lean on the rim of the pit and who should goggle over their shoulders; did it depend on how much they'd paid for admission? Several of the customers were rather handsomely dressed, with shiny buttons on their coats, immaculate hats, fashionable cravats that cost fifty times more than the grubby cotton scarf worn by the rat-catcher. Clara doubted these gentlemen would ever set foot in a place like The Traveller's Rest, were it not for the scuffling, squeaking contents of the keg.

'All right, gentlemen,' announced the publican when Mr Heaton had disappeared into an anteroom beyond the cellar. 'We have two dogs this afternoon, Robbie and Lopsy-Lou. Less rats than we might've hoped. How shall we divvy up the day's proceedings?'

This provoked a roisterous babble of bets and disputation.

'A shilling on Robbie to kill five in fifteen seconds!'

'Two shillings on Lopsy-Lou to kill twenty in fifty seconds!'

'Here's a shilling says twelve of twenty's still kicking after half a minute!'

'If we've only got seventy-five rats, it should be three matches of twenty-five each.'

'That muddles everything!'

'Twenty is a good number.'

'It don't go into seventy-five.'

'All my bets is calculated on twenty.'

'We know all about your bets. You expect to see blood for sixpence.'

'We can't have three matches with only two dogs.'

''Course we can. Best of three.'

'Put out thirty-seven rats each match, and god damn the one left over!'

'Lopsy-Lou is heavier than Robbie; she should have a handicap. I say Robbie kills ten for Lopsy's fifteen.'

'Why should a Manchester terrier have it easier than a London one?'

'Let's weigh the dogs! Each kills as many rats as he weighs in pounds. The dog that kills his quota quickest is the winner.'

'I don't see no scales.'

'A public house with no scales?'

'Keep the times and rats the same number, but give Robbie smaller rats!'

'What bollocks! If he can't kill his share, he shouldn't be here!'

'Why not set a fixed time – half a minute, say – and see which dog kills the most?'

'I won't bet dog against dog. It should be dog against rat.'

'Anyway, what would you do after the thirty seconds was up, and there was still rats alive?'

'Pull the dog out of the pit, of course.'

'That's cruel!'

'Gentlemen!' barked the publican. 'We must begin. Let's have twenty in the pit for Robbie and see how the first match pleases you.'

This seemed to satisfy the majority, and the bets were swiftly laid, and the money collected. During this process, Mr Heaton emerged from the shadows, holding his dog by a leash, very close to its collar. It was indeed a beautiful dog, a silky black animal, somewhat smaller than Clara had anticipated. It was placid, standing patiently at its master's side, looking up at him for approval – until the publican opened the lid of the barrel and started doling rats into the pit. Then Robbie reared up, lunging against the leash, and Mr Heaton had to pull him hard against his thigh.

The publican worked swiftly but carefully. Using a pair of metal tongs designed for removing buns from an oven, he selected the squirming rodents one by one from the keg, and deposited them gently into the pit. The rats (a little various in size, which caused mutters of complaint among the spectators) seemed healthy specimens of their kind, as sleek as kittens and as nimble as cockroaches. They immediately attempted to scuttle to freedom, but the sides of the pit were smooth, and the pit's rim had a lip of metal screwed onto it for extra security. The sound of tiny claws scrabbling against polished wood was marvellously distinctive. The way the rats slid back down to the chalk-whitened floor was comical. Clara licked her lips.

Mr Heaton made his way, with some difficulty, to her side. His limp was one problem, the barely suppressed frenzy of poor Robbie another. The dog was making little whining sounds, deep in its throat — plaintive whore noises. Seventeen, eighteen, nineteen rats had been doled out into the pit. Mr Heaton stood close to Clara, his hip almost touching her waist. The unscarred parts of his face were shiny with sweat, and the muscles in his neck were bulging, a phenomenon with which Clara, in her new profession, had become increasingly familiar. The moment was almost nigh.

At the drop of the twentieth rat into the ring, a tall man with a stopwatch started a short countdown to Robbie's release. Those five seconds were the longest Clara had ever endured.

The instant the dog's collar was unfastened, he shot into the pit and began killing rats. Contrary to Clara's expectations, he didn't chase them round and round the enclosure, feinting and dodging and hesitating like a cat with a mouse. He killed with the efficiency of a machine. The rats swarmed helplessly to and fro, clustering together in corners of the octagonal arena, or dashing across to the opposite side. The dog didn't waste time chasing individuals. He pounced on groups, picking off the rat nearest him, dispatching the squealing creature with a single bite. One snap of his jaws seemed enough. He didn't bother even to give his kill a triumphal shake, but merely let it drop to the floor as soon as his teeth had stabbed through the soft flesh.

With a dawning thrill of admiration, Clara realised there was more to the dog's performance than random brutality: he paced his exertions with extraordinary cunning, pausing for a half a second here and there to allow stray rats to huddle together again, stamping one paw on the ground to dissuade a rat from running the wrong way. His eyes were bright with a fierce intelligence. There was some-thing weirdly benign about his murderousness; he treated each rat the same, neglected none. He killed with a conscience, clearly aware of the bets placed upon him, the high hopes of his master.

Twelve rats dead, thirteen, fourteen. Mr Heaton was hard up against Clara, his arm nudging hers. The cellar was delirious with desperate noises: heavy breathing, the squeals and skitterings of doomed rats, the taloned patter of dog feet, hoarse cries of 'Yes!' and 'There!'

It was over all too soon. Robbie lunged at the last rat, broke its back with a snap of his jaws. A great cheer went up, and the time-keeper punched his fist in the air. Clara gasped, slumped against the rim of the rat pit, whose metal surface she found she was gripping with both hands.

The aftermath was messy. Not because of blood or saliva (Robbie had been remarkably clean) but because there was disagreement among the spectators over the deadness of some of the rats. A forlorn specimen was fished from the ring and laid on the floor at the men's feet. One man alleged that the creature only had its back broken, rendering it immobile, but that it was still alive: he had seen it choke for breath. Another man stamped on the rat's tail, arguing that if it had any life left in it, the pain would surely summon up some reaction. There was none. A second contentious rat was retrieved from the arena, having allegedly been spotted breathing. Although limp and unconscious, it seemed to be very much alive; its abdomen was palpating visibly. Two of the men who had bet against Robbie insisted that he'd failed to kill his quota. Another man proposed that the match be resumed just for a few seconds, to allow Robbie to kill this last rat in whatever time it took – to which the two dissenters objected that it would obviously take the dog only half a second to kill a rat which was insensible, but that he ought to've done the job properly the first time. The rat-catcher, who had been regarding the creature philosophically all this while, suddenly bent down and slit open the rat's belly with a knife. A grisly sight was revealed: a tangle of foetal sacs, shiny as sausages, each containing a squirming baby rat, fully-furred and almost ready for life.

''Ave we got a puppy wants to learn a trade?' quipped the rat-catcher, and the good spirits of the company were restored.

With one exception. Mr Heaton left The Traveller's Rest before Lopsy-Lou even had her chance to perform. He pleaded a stomach upset, and indeed he did look ghastly, his face a mixture of bone-white and beefsteak red. His fellow sportsmen protested that he must stay: Robbie was a champion and would surely be given a third match after Lopsy-Lou had done her dash. Lopsy-Lou's owner hinted that Mr Heaton's sudden illness might indicate a greater regard for his already-pocketed winnings than for the inherent value of watching two noble dogs compete. But Mr Heaton was not to be persuaded. His digestion, he insisted, was very bad. He shouldn't be a bit surprised if he was in bed within the hour.

Without speaking to each other, Mr Heaton and Clara walked side-by-side out of the pub. Mr Heaton hailed a cab at once, and for a moment Clara was afraid he would leave her standing on the footpath while he sped away. But he opened the cabin door for her, with stony-faced courtesy, and waited for her to climb in.

'You broke your promise,' he said, as soon as they were seated and the vehicle was in motion.

'I forgot, sir,' she said.

'I reminded you,' he said. 'Twice.'

'I couldn't take my eyes off the dog and the rats, sir. It was my first time.'

He sighed deeply, and looked out the window. Night was falling. Shopworkers were hurrying home. A lamplighter was doing what seemed like callisthenics, stretching his back and arms in preparation for the task ahead.

'I'm sorry, sir,' said Clara. She surmised that Mr Heaton was too much of a gentleman to demand his ten shillings back, but thought it was just as well to show contrition, so that he might take pity on her.

'What's done is done,' he said, in a tone of bitter melancholy. He seemed to be retreating into a world of his own, a place where he alone could go. Clara found this more discomfiting than if he had loudly chastised her in the street.

'I'm sorry, sir,' she said again, peeking surreptitiously at whether he was softening towards her. He appeared not to have heard.

The cab joined the traffic bound for Westminster, rattled across the bridge, passed the houses of Parliament. The tall buildings blocked out the sun, bringing on the night all the quicker. Mr Heaton unfastened his overcoat, unbuttoned the coat he wore underneath, and pulled out a tobacco tin from an inside pocket. He rolled himself a cigarette and lit it. Inhaling for what seemed like a very long time, he tilted his head back against the back wall of the cabin. It was then that Clara saw the deep scar on his neck, just under his beard-line, running almost from earlobe to earlobe. The scar was perfectly semi-circular in shape, except for a hiccup caused by the Adam's apple. It was punctuated all around by other scars: cross-shaped white dots where someone had crudely stitched the gaping flesh back together. The dots looked as if buttons had once been sewn there and fallen off unnoticed.

'What happened to you, sir?' Clara asked.

He exhaled smoke until it hung around his head like a fog. He stared up at the ceiling, blinking his gleaming, bloodshot eyes.

'Happened?' he murmured absently.

'Someone hurt you, sir.' She pointed at his neck, almost touching him. He smiled but didn't respond.

'Was it robbers, sir?'

Again he smiled. 'You might say that.' He took the deepest possible puff of his cigarette, making it glow fierce in the dimness of the cabin.

The hansom rattled on. Through the window on her side, Clara saw a landmark she recognised from that lost period of her life when she used to meet with another lady's maid called Sinead at a tea-room near Charing Cross Station. She knew where she was now, more or less. It wouldn't be very long before they were back in St Giles, so she started rehearsing what her parting words to Mr Heaton ought to be, whether she should affect a breezy tone or a solemn one; whether a third apology might melt him or whether she'd milked contrition for as much as it was worth; whether she ought to suggest that they attempt to do this again next month, despite her honest intention never to clap eyes on him again. Just when she was deep in thought, debating the wisdom of perhaps giving him some sort of kiss on the cheek the instant before sprinting to her freedom, he spoke again.

'I was in the Battle of Peiwar Kotal.'

'How terrible, sir. Was that in India?'

'Afghanistan.'

Clara had never heard of the place. Admittedly her schooling had been scant and she'd entered into service almost immediately afterward, and her mistress, for all her wealth, knew nothing about anything. Clara strained to recall if Mr William Rackham, her mistress's husband, had ever uttered any informative pronouncements about Afghanistan in her earshot. But thinking of the pompous windbag who'd dismissed her with a damning letter of reference – a letter of reference so poisonous that she'd spent more than three years trying to get decent employment with it, only to be driven to her current line of work – made her deaf, dumb and blind with anger.

'I don't know much about history, sir,' she said.

He flicked his cigarette out of the window. 'It was last year, actually.' Turning his face close to hers, he examined her features as though evaluating, for the first time, her desirability as a woman. 'You think I'm an old man, don't you? I'm younger than *you* are, I'll wager.'

'I wouldn't wager against you, sir.'

He broke off his gaze and slumped back in his seat. His melancholy pout and wispy beard struck her, all of a sudden, as boyish. He was fine-boned and slender, after all. Whatever he'd endured in battle had added ten, twenty, thirty years onto his age.

'How did the war start, sir?'

He chuckled, an ugly sound. 'The leader of the Afghans, Shere Ali, made friends with a Russian gentleman. Our government decided that this friendship was not in the interests of our empire. So several thousand men, including myself, marched from India to Afghanistan. When we reached the Peiwar Pass, we were met with an army of eighteen thousand Afghans.'

'Oh, heavens, sir: what a terrible defeat you suffered.'

He laughed again. 'Defeat? On the contrary: we won. That is, Her Majesty's army won. I, personally, did not win. As you can see.'

Clara chewed her lower lip, feeling wretchedly out of her depth.

'It's awful, sir. We should all be thankful to you, sir, for the victory.'

He was rummaging in his clothing for the tobacco tin. 'It's a little too soon to celebrate, I'm afraid,' he said, as he began to construct another cigarette. 'The war goes on.'

'Goes on, sir?'

'I was wounded in a battle. The war goes on. Only a month ago, we lost hundreds of men in a disastrous defeat in Maiwand.'

Clara was silent. If there was a lesson to be learned from this fiasco, it was never to participate in conversations she could not hope to keep her place in. While Mr Heaton made short work of his cigarette, Clara simmered with frustration; she wished she could somehow make him understand that she had suffered, too. She wanted to tell him all about her unfair dismissal, and the many humiliations that had preceded it, and the insults she had endured after it, and, most of all, the indignities she had been forced to undergo at the hands of those swinish, repulsive creatures, the men who used whores. She held her tongue.

Familiar lights were glowing in the distance. Night had descended entirely, and the temperature in the cabin had become chilly. Clara became aware that her hands were still bare. She fetched her gloves out of the pocket of her dress, taking great care not to jingle the coins in there. But in attempting to put her right glove on, she discovered that the nail of her middle finger was impeding progress more than usual: it was jagged, shaped like the edge of a specialised cutting-tool. She must have gripped the rim of the rat pit harder than she remembered.

An unexpected voice – her own – piped up in the dark.

'My nail is broken, sir. But it's still quite long. And very sharp. Do you want to feel it, sir?'

She put her hand into the murky space between them and he took it. She dug her fingernail into his palm, to demonstrate its potentials.

'Shall I, sir?'

He wrapped her finger in his hand, holding it gently.

'It's all right,' he said. 'Not now.'

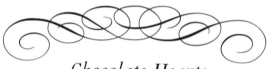

*Chocolate Hearts*
*from the New World*

n the professional judgement of Dr James Curlew, his unfortunate daughter had, at the very most, five years left before it was all over. Not her life, you understand; her prospects for marriage. The same physical features that made him such a distinguished-looking man – tall, rangy build, aquiline nose, long face, strong jaw – were a calamitous inheritance for a girl. If she acted quickly, now while she was in her teens, there was still hope.

'Oh, but I don't wish to marry, Father,' she told him. 'The world has enough married folk in it. What it hasn't got enough of is missionaries.'

'In that case,' he joked, 'it's damn naughty of the savages in Africa to keep eating them, isn't it?'

'You mustn't call them savages, Father,' Emmeline chided him solemnly. 'Such disparagements are precisely why slavery is still with us.'

Dr Curlew clenched his jaw – the same jaw he'd passed on to his blameless daughter – and did his best not to argue. Rancour between him and

Emmeline would have grieved his wife, had she lived to see it.

'I don't know why you say "still with us",' he couldn't help remarking. 'We don't have slavery in England.'

'We must regard the whole world as our home, Father,' said Emmeline, wiping her fingers on the breakfast napkin. Pale sunlight was shining through the parlour window onto her face and upper body, a cool glow aided by the white tablecloth and the snowy landscape outside. The jingling of horses' harnesses as the nearby shops received their deliveries mingled with the tinkling of Emmeline's spoon in her teacup. 'This is the 1850s,' she reminded her father, as if the modern age had arrived while he'd been occupied else-where. 'Every place on Earth is connected by the web of our Empire. I have correspondents as far-flung as Kabool and New York.'

'Oh?' This was promising. Without taking his eyes off his daughter, he rang the bell for the housemaid, as the room wasn't as warm as it should be. 'Might some of these correspondents be of the male sex?'

'Oh, the majority of them, Father,' grinned Emmeline. 'Males are in far more desperate need of salvation than females, I've found.'

She was quite winsome when she smiled. Her lips still had something of the childish rosebud about them, and there were dimples in her cheeks. Her eyes were bright, her face unlined, her hair glossy. Five years, at most, she would retain these qualities, then the sap would begin to drain out of her, and she would be left only with the aquiline nose and the Curlew jaw. Moreover, arithmetic would be against her; she would strike any potential suitors as unfeasibly old. Dear little Emmeline could prattle all she liked about modern Society and how unrecognisably different it was from when he was a young man, but some attitudes were eternal.

The maidservant padded into the room and, without needing to be told, perceived at once what the trouble was. She got on her knees in front of the hearth and started coaxing the flames. Worth her weight in gold, that girl.

Once Emmeline had declared that she was writing to many mysterious gentlemen all over the world, her father was naturally curious to know if this were true, and, if so, who these mysterious gentlemen might be. Emmeline was clearly not going to tell him, so he had a word with Gertie who, in addition to her

other duties, also had the task of walking to the pil-
larbox to post Miss Curlew's letters.

'Yes, sir,' said the servant. 'Never less than one
a day. Sometimes five or six.'

'Always to the same person?'

'No, sir.'

'Replies?'

'Sometimes, sir.'

'From . . . from what part of the world, usually?'

'America, sir.'

'How tantalising.'

'Yes, sir.'

In point of fact, most of the letters that Emmeline
sent went unanswered. She tried to write at least half
a dozen each afternoon, but sometimes her wrist
grew weak or she got the urge to go out walking. It
really would be a great boon to mankind (and wom-
ankind!) if someone could invent a mechanism for
making automatic copies of a page of text. All this
fuss in the newspapers recently about Mr Sobrero
inventing nitro-glycerine! What did the world need
another method of destruction for, when there were
all sorts of useful things yet to be invented? However,
she would scribble on regardless. There was a war

to be fought – her own just and gentle war. The war against slavery.

The gentlemen to whom she wrote were mainly located in Louisiana, Missouri, Alabama, Mississippi, Tennessee, Kentucky, Arkansas, Georgia, Florida, the Virginias and the Carolinas. Modifying a generic text with a sprinkling of local details gleaned from imported newspapers and journals, she would address each man as well-informedly as she could, imploring him to renounce slave-owning and allow his hard heart to be penetrated by the love of Christ. She quoted passages of Scripture. She quoted Charles Dickens's *American Notes*. She hinted that if the recipient should be inspired to recant his sinful behaviour and set his slaves free, there would, in this world, exist at least one person – Miss Emmeline Curlew – who would venerate him as a hero. Moral courage, she argued, is the manliest of virtues, and few men possess it.

Most of these letters vanished into a void. A small proportion provoked replies, slim envelopes arriving weeks and months afterwards, single sheets suffused with varying strengths of nasty temper.

*I will thank you to keep your ignorant and impudent babblings to yourself,* said one.

*Has it occurred to you, Miss,* said another, *that the very clothes you are wearing as you pen your imperious missive may have their origins in my cotton fields?*

*Our postal system,* averred another, *is superior to yours, but it may not long remain so if it is burdened with unsolicited and mischievous piffle.*

Some respondents went to greater effort, quoting passages from the Bible apparently condoning slavery, and wishing Miss Curlew a measure of wisdom and tolerance of other folks' customs as she grew older. One man in Port Hudson said that if she spent half an hour in the company of the niggers she spoke of so glowingly, the brutes would make her wish she'd never been born, and then most likely murder her. She even received one letter from a plantation-owner's wife, threatening her with hellfire, hired assassins and savage dogs if 'you damned English hussy' dared to write to her husband again.

*May our Lord forgive you,* Emmeline wrote back, *for your unkind and, if I may say so, blasphemous words . . .*

One day, a most unusual item of mail was delivered. The bulk of the Curlews' correspondence arrived at their house either in the first post, early in the morning, or in the last post, at evening. This item arrived at midday, while Emmeline and her father were being served luncheon. It was a handsomely wrapped box, on which the sender had affixed slightly insufficient postage. Dr Curlew had to pay the postman ninepence, and his brow was wrinkled as he carried the parcel into the parlour. He wasn't acquainted with anyone in Chickamauga, Georgia.

'It's for you,' he said, handing it over to his daughter.

Emmeline laid the parcel in the lap of her skirts, and returned her attention to the cold galantine on her plate. She carved off another slice and conveyed it to her mouth, her big jaw swinging down as she did so.

'Aren't you curious to see what it is?' said Dr Curlew.

The girl chewed, swallowed. 'Of course I'm curious.'

'So am I. Would it be very presumptuous if I asked you to open it now?'

'Yes, it would, Father,' smiled Emmeline, 'but I forgive you.' And she fetched the package up onto the table and tore its layers of brown paper off. Inside were a letter, a photograph and a box of chocolates. The letter and photograph Emmeline laid unexamined behind the teapot. The chocolates she opened for her father's inspection.

'Very fancy,' he commented, extracting, from under the powdered paper cups of dark, luxurious-smelling confectionery, a slip of paper detailing the varieties. The slip of paper itself was impregnated with a delicious aroma, and he sniffed it briefly before studying what it had to say. Terms like 'delectable', 'exotic', 'rich' and 'luscious' recurred throughout.

'Who is this gentleman?' enquired Dr Curlew, laying the paper over the glittering assortment of pralines and caramels.

Emmeline fetched up the letter and frowned at the signature.

'I'm not sure,' she said. 'I have so many. I must have read about him in an article somewhere.'

'The photograph – is it of him?'

Emmeline picked up the thick rectangle of card.

'I presume so. I can't recall ever seeing this face before.' After a moment's hesitation she handed the photograph to her father. He studied it just as he had studied the fragrant slip of paper.

'Presentable-looking chap,' he conceded. 'Upright carriage, broad shoulders. Firm jaw. Healthy, I expect. His trousers could use a press. But not a bad specimen.' Dr Curlew was keeping his tone as calm and offhand as he could, but in truth he was already picturing the offspring of this union. A grandson, maybe even two. Fine, robust boys, calling him grandpa in barbarous accents.

'A remarkably . . . amiable gesture on his part, sending you these chocolates,' he observed.

Emmeline gestured across the table. Her hand was, as always, somewhat ink-stained. 'Do have one, Father.'

'Thank you, I will.' And he popped a hazelnut-encrusted globe into his mouth, allowing it to melt against his palate while his daughter read the letter in silence.

*Dear Miss Curlew,*

*Thank you for your letter. May I say that you have the most elegant handwriting? Quite a change from that produced by any of the ladies here. Your signature especially caused me to linger over it, admiring its combination of simplicity, confidence & grace. Less refined females imagine that a paroxism of calligraphic flourishes consigns elegance upon them. It takes a signature such as yours to make clear the gulf between the genuine article & its imitations.*

*However, you will be growing impatient with these flatteries (however sincerely meant). You wish to know what I thought of your advice to me. You hope, perhaps, for news that I have freed my slaves & dedicated myself to Christ. On the latter matter I can reassure you; I love our Lord as much as any decent, imperfect man can. The passages you quoted from the Good Book are of course well known to me, as are other passages which take a different position.*

*As far as my slaves are concerned, they are free already. That is, I give them as much freedom as good sense allows, & care for them as conscientiously as I would my own children (of whom, sadly, I have none). My slaves are contented and healthy; their duties are not onerous. The climate in Georgia is rather more salubrious than you may be accustomed to in England, and the crops grow with little fuss, ripening in the glorious sun that God has seen fit to shine over my modest domain. As I pen these words, Perry, one of my field hands, is playing with Shakespeare, my dog. He does this not because he is obliged to but because he likes Shakespeare and, if you will forgive me boasting, is fond of his master too. In fact, if slavery should ever be abolished — as I fear it will be, if the strident voices in our own Northern states exchange their shouting for bellicose action — I am worried for my poor Perry. He is a trusting & gentle creature, and if he is forced to make his own way in this cruel world, without so much as a roof over his head, I suspect he will suffer a dismal fate.*

*I do not expect that these few words will convince you of the rightness of my way of life. I regret that you cannot visit my home & make your own judgements. I can only hope that if you were, by some miracle, to arrive as my esteemed guest, you would find this place to be a happy & pleasant one, lacking only the charm that a mistress might have provided, had not my fiancée been taken from me in tragic circumstances.*

*I can assure you that, far from being the hotbed of savagery and squalor that you may imagine, Georgia is really quite a civilised place. It even has a chocolate shop, as you have no doubt already divined. I offer you these sweet trifles as a token of my gratitude for your interest in my soul. A poor gift, I know; some might say an impertinent one. But since you already possess a Bible, the most precious gift any of us can own, it is difficult to imagine what else you might possibly need. Chocolates can, at least, give pleasure, & if you don't eat them, you can always give them to your parents.*

*With my most cordial best wishes . . .*

Emmeline looked up from her reading.

'Well?' said her father. 'What's your opinion of this fellow?'

Emmeline folded the letter in her strong fingers and wedged it under the saucer of her teacup. Then she gazed past her father's shoulder at the snow-frosted window, her eyes half-closed. The grey terraced houses of Bayswater, the iron lamp-posts and the hearse-like delivery carts, had lost some of their solidity for her; they were semi-transparent, shifting ephemera in a monochrome kaleidoscope.

'He can't spell "paroxysm" or "conscientiously",' she remarked, in a faraway tone. Her eyes grew more and more unfocused. She was picturing the lush fields of Georgia, endless acres of fertility. Her man's property was a vast bed of soft green enlivened with ripe cotton, a wholly mysterious substance she imagined resembling snow-white poppies. And, standing erect in the middle of those fields, his hands on his hips, there he was, silhouetted against the cloudless sky, his outline shimmering in the heat. An ecstatic dog ran up to him, leaping against his chest, licking his neck, and he embraced it, laughing. To the far left, in the corner of her mind's eye, stood a dark figure, a Negro bearing an uncanny resemblance to an illustration in

*Dred: A Tale of the Great Dismal Swamp*, one of several novels by Harriet Beecher Stowe in Emmeline's book-case. 'Anyway,' she added, 'he keeps slaves.'

Dr Curlew harrumphed. 'Is that the only reason you wrote to him?'

Emmeline blinked, looked away from the window, returned home to England.

'Have another chocolate, Father,' she said.

'Might you perhaps write to him again?' asked Dr Curlew. 'Or is he past saving?'

Emmeline lowered her head and smiled, blushing a little.

'No one is past saving, Father,' she replied, and fetched up the letter and photograph. The mute form of Gertie was hovering in the doorway, waiting for permission to clear the table. Luncheon had run overtime; Dr Curlew must call upon his patients, and Miss Curlew must retire to her bedroom, her favoured place, always, for correspondence.

The Fly, and Its Effect
upon Mr Bodley

rs Tremain opens the door of her house in Fitzrovia, to find a formally dressed, bleary-eyed, somewhat desperate-looking man standing on the threshold. This is not unusual in itself, although eleven o'clock in the morning is rather early for the first customer. Most men who get a hankering for a whore before midday pick one off the street and conduct their business in an alley, especially on these balmy summer days when no one is likely to catch a chill. Only in the evenings, when gentlemen have been drinking port and reading pornography in their clubs, and when a sumptuous meal has turned their thoughts to cigars and fellatio, does Mrs Tremain's house become a bustling attraction.

'Why, Mr Bodley!' she exclaims delightedly. 'Where is Mr Ashwell?'

As all the best prostitutes in London know, Mr Bodley and Mr Ashwell are inseparable. Not in the sense of being Sodomites, for they are happy enough to trot into different rooms when each of them has been given a suitable female companion. But they are chums. They confer in all things, including the choice of brothel, the choice of wine, the choice of girl, and afterwards they compare their findings.

'Ashwell is asleep, I expect,' mutters Mr Bodley. 'As all self-respecting men-about-town should be at this time of day.'

'Some of us are early risers, Mr Bodley,' says Mrs Tremain, motioning her guest to step inside. 'You will find half the girls are available to you immediately, and all but one of them within half an hour, if you can bear to wait.'

'Wait?' says Mr Bodley mournfully. 'I can wait forever. I shouldn't have come. I should be at home in bed. I should be in my grave. My whoring days are over.'

'Oh, don't say that, sir. Come see what we have for you.'

Mrs Tremain takes him to the parlour, where two young ladies are seated on the floor, barefoot, dressed only in their undergarments. Their white petticoats puddle all around them, touching at the hems. Their corsets are loose, sagging off their naked shoulders, the loose clasps glittering. Their hair is up, but untidy. They smell of stale perfume, soap and strawberries (a red-stained straw punnet lies discarded and empty in the corner, indicating the street-market origin of their breakfast). In the morning light the lack the erotic allure lent by lamp-lit shadows, and instead look domesticated, like a litter of puppies.

Girl Number One is a pale, freckled lass whom Bodley vaguely remembers having tried once before. Girl Number Two is wholly unfamiliar to him, a sloe-eyed Asiatic with lustrous black hair.

'Mr Bodley, meet our newest,' says Mrs Tremain. 'She is from the Malay Straits. Her name is something like Pang or Ping, but we call her Lily. Lily, stand up and greet the gentleman.'

Nudged under the elbow by Girl Number One, Lily scrambles to her feet, and curtseys. She is perhaps four foot eleven, but very beautiful.

'Fuck, sir. Fuck,' she says, brightly.

'We are teaching her English, sir,' says Girl Number One, 'beginning with the essentials.'

Lily curtseys again. 'Fucky fuck, sir. Fucky fuck fuck.'

'Charming,' says Mr Bodley.

'Fucky fuck muck-a-muck wuck.'

Girl Number One smirks, and pulls at Lily's skirts, signalling her to sit down. 'We've not had much time, sir, to teach her. But she's powerful willing.'

Mr Bodley nods, then turns his face theatrically towards the heavily curtained window, his jaw set hard.

'The willingness of comely girls, the novelty of foreign flesh, the smell of strawberries — none of these things can mean anything to me now.'

'Oh dear,' says Mrs Tremain. 'Is it as bad as that?'

'Worse, worse,' sighs Mr Bodley, perching his bottom on the armrest of a chaise longue, and resting his palms on his knees. Disconsolately he stares at the Persian rug under his polished shoes. 'In this house, the candleflame of my manhood was snuffed out.'

Mrs Tremain takes a deep breath, licks her lips, and comes out with it.

'You haven't a complaint about us, I trust, sir?'

'A complaint?' says Bodley. 'No, no, madam. I have always found your house to be hospitable in the extreme. Although . . .' (he looks towards the curtained window again, his face stoical in grief) 'something unfortunate did happen here last time

I availed myself of your hospitality. What bearing it has on my current state of distress, I cannot say for certain.'

'Distress? Oh, mercy, sir: I don't like to hear that. Not from a valued customer such as yourself. You didn't use Bella, I hope?'

'Why? Is there some problem with Bella?'

'Not any more, sir. She's gone.'

'I don't believe I ever had Bella.'

'Just as well, sir.'

'Although . . . what would have happened if I had?'

'Nothing untoward, sir. We use only the best, the purest, the friendliest, the healthiest and the delight-fullest girls here, sir. Until they cease to be so. Then they must go elsewhere.'

Girl Number One examines her fingernails. Lily leans over to see what is so remarkable about them.

'I believe it was Minnie I had,' says Mr Bodley, his brow wrinkling with the effort of recalling the name.

'A paragon, sir,' affirms Mrs Tremain. 'No part of her falls beneath perfection.'

'Indeed not, indeed not. Only, I could not help noticing . . . when she was positioned before me, on her hands and knees, with her dress pulled up to expose her arse-hole and cunt, for we had not yet established which of these I would select . . .'

'Yes?'

'A fly settled on her left buttock.'

'A fly, sir?'

'A common fly. A fly such as one sees buzzing around a fruit stall in the street.'

Mrs Tremain blinks slowly. The temperature in the room is rising gently as the day advances.

'Well, it *is* summer, sir,' she reminds her guest. 'There are millions of flies about. Is it really so miraculous that one of them should have got into our house?'

'No, not at all.'

'We keep a clean house, sir. The Queen's palace won't be as clean, I'll wager. But we must keep it ventilated, sir. That's part of good health: ventilation. And where there's an open window, a fly may enter. And even be so bold as to settle on a girl's behind.'

'Understood, madam. I don't mean to criticise . . .'

'The fly didn't crawl somewhere it shouldn't, I hope? I mean, somewhere that might have come between you and your pleasure?'

'No, no, no. It flew off at my approach. Minnie and I were soon conjoined. I was fully satisfied, and in fact paid her extra.'

'And yet today you are distressed?'

Mr Bodley embraces himself with his arms, and inclines his head pensively to one side.

'I've been thinking, madam. About that fly. About flies in general. Flies feed on rotting matter. They lay eggs in it. The maggots that decompose us when we are dead are laid by flies.'

'I assure you Minnie is very much alive, sir. She's in the bath just now, but if you were to give her fifteen minutes, I'm sure she would be able to demonstrate to you that she is frisky and entirely maggot-free.'

'Yes, but that's exactly it, don't you see? We are alive for but a fleeting moment. Millions have lived and died before us, millions will come after us, and for what?'

Mrs Tremain's shoulders slump visibly, despite the puff sleeves of her dress. It's five past eleven in the morning, far too early to solve the libertine's recurrent crisis of will.

'I'm a purveyor of pleasure, sir, not a clergyman. However, I can assure you that we have plenty of clergymen coming here. A man can spend only so much time pondering Death before he gets an appetite for other things.'

'Well, my appetite is gone. Quite gone.'

Mrs Tremain regards Mr Bodley for a few seconds, taking his measure. Then she winks towards Lily, saying, 'Would you consider a few minutes with Lily, sir, free of charge? If she fails to kindle your . . . your candleflame, we shall know how serious the problem is. If – as I'm confident will be the case – you are quickened to action, the price will still be reasonable. Lily is inexperienced, after all.'

'Fucky fuck fuck,' Lily pipes up.

'No, no, really I couldn't,' groans Mr Bodley. 'What would be the point? Even if my flesh were to respond according to its animal design? I am a normal, robust man, this girl has lips and tongue and all the rest of it. There is no impediment to our carnal competence. Except its sheer pointlessness, madam. I have performed this act thousands of times before.'

'As have *we*, sir,' Mrs Tremain reminds him, but he is lost in his own lamentations.

'Thousands of copulations. Thousands of repetitions of the same motions. The stroking of necks and cheeks. The baring of the breasts. The unclothing of the hindquarters. Ministrations to ensure the cunt's lubricity; ministrations to ensure the cock's rigidity. Always the same sequence of frustration, negotiation, expectation, capitulation, then, uh . . .'

'Release? Rapture?'

'Alleviation.'

Mrs Tremain sniffs. 'You are an idealist, sir, and your idealism is making you miserable. Most of us manage to find joy in routine pleasures. Like eating, sleeping . . .'

Mr Bodley snorts irritably. 'I've been sleeping damn little lately.'

'Ah, there you may have your problem, sir,' remarks Mrs Tremain, suddenly inspired. 'Sleep is essential for the soul's good health. I make sure all my girls get a portion of sleep every night. Otherwise they'd go mad, I'm sure. Which may be what's happening to you, sir, if I may be so bold.'

'No, I have merely stared deep into the abyss of human futility . . .'

'How did you spend last night, if you don't mind me asking, sir?'

Mr Bodley reacts as if someone has just flicked his nose.

'Last night? Uh . . . I spent it with Ashwell. We

went to a rat-fight in Whitechapel, almost got ourselves murdered. Then we found a place to drink,
and drank. Then the sun came up and I caught a cab
home. Unable to recall the location of my bedroom,
I dozed for perhaps an hour in my vestibule. Then a
volley of letters was pushed through the mail slot in
my front door and hit me on the face.'

'And the night before?'

Mr Bodley frowns with the effort of penetrating
so far back into history.

'I was with Ashwell again. We went to Mrs
Foscoe's in Brompton Road. Ashwell promised me
that two of our old dons from Cambridge would be
there, getting whipped. They never came, but we
had to get whipped while waiting; it would've been
impolite not to. Then I had a little accident which
required immediate attention. Ashwell said he knew
a doctor, a good friend of his, in Beaufort Gardens.
But we were so drunk, we ended up in Hyde Park,
and I fell into the Serpentine while attempting to
wash. Then . . . uh . . . my memory is indistinct.
Something involving horses, I think, and a
policeman.'

'I suppose you slept much of the next day, sir?'

'Scarcely a wink. I had to go see my father, to

explain certain matters arising from a publishing ven-
ture of mine. Also, the people upstairs have bought
a dog, a very argumentative dog whose throat I have
not yet found time to cut.'

'I see,' says Mrs Tremain. Indeed, she observes
that her guest's eyes are bloodshot and that his hands
are trembling.

'But these are trifles,' groans Mr Bodley. 'Mere
flotsam on the vast accumulated ocean of pointless
endeavour. All human satisfactions are lost to me.'

'Just mislaid, I'm sure, sir,' says Mrs Tremain, in
her most soothingly maternal tone. 'The sleep's the
main thing, I believe. You are weary, terribly weary,
I see that now, sir. Wouldn't you like to lie down in
one of our spare beds? We'd barely charge you, sir.
A night's sleep for the price of a glass of good wine.'

Mr Bodley stares stupidly at her. His lower lip
swells, making him look like a boy of six.

'I haven't a nightgown with me,' he protests
feebly.

'Sleep naked, sir. Our beds are warm, and it's
summer.'

'I can't sleep without a nightgown,' says Bodley,
covering his eyes with his tremulous hands. 'It's not
natural.'

'Very well, sir.' Mrs Tremain gestures at Girl Number One, a complex mime with wrist and fingers. Girl Number One jumps up and hurries from the room, returning within moments holding a white nightshift.

'Oh, but really . . . !' Mr Bodley begins to protest, as the feminine garment is unfurled before him.

'You won't know the difference, sir, when you're asleep. On a luxurious, soft pillow, sir, in a darkened room, in a house full of languorous women, and no dogs.'

Mr Bodley somewhat resembles a dog himself, gazing in hope at his mistress. Before his shame can overcome him, he reaches for the nightgown and gathers it to his chest.

'Take Mr Bodley to bed, dear,' says Mrs Tremain to Girl Number One.

Mr Bodley shambles towards the stairs, led by the girl whose name he still can't recall, and whose nightgown he is about to wear. 'Much obliged,' he mumbles. 'But I am sleeping unaccompanied, do we understand one another? The bed is for that purpose only. Yes?'

'Yes, sir,' says Girl Number One.

'Fucky fuck bed-sleep, sir,' says Lily.

'Good morning, sir,' says Mrs Tremain.

'Good night, ladies,' says Mr Bodley. 'Sweet ladies, good night.'

The Apple

n Mrs Castaway's brothel, at an hour of morning when decent folk are already awake and busy, Sugar is roused from a deep sleep by the sound of an urgent voice. It's not in the room with her, thank God. It's coming from down below, from the mews behind the house, where only horses, drunks and thieves usually go. The voice is singing, serenading her, right under her window.

*To Hell with you*, Sugar thinks, and covers her head with a pillow.

The voice sings on. It is not the voice of the man who shared her bed last night. He's lost in his own drunken slumber miles away from here, hidden inside his respectable, fragrant family home. No, this is a woman's voice, fruity and righteous.

> *Dark and cheerless is the morn*
> *Unaccompanied by Thee . . .*

Sugar groans. The morn is nowhere near as dark as she'd like it to be: sunlight streams through the windowpane, winkling her out of her sweet oblivion. The pillow over her head is no help at all, nor does the extra swaddling provided by her fleecy hair make any difference. Worse, the pillowcase stinks horribly of a man's hair-oil, despite the fact that her last customer was dispatched sixteen hours ago; if she presses the pillow any harder against her face she'll suffocate. And still the singing penetrates, only slightly muffled by the cotton and the feathers.

*Oh happy house! supremely blest!*
*Where Christ is entertained*
*as its most dear-beloved guest*
*with selfless love unfeigned.*

Sugar tosses the pillow aside, blinking in the golden glare. An evangelist! A female evangelist! Here in Silver Street, Soho! Is this woman stupider than most, or cleverer? To sing about Christ being entertained with selfless love, right outside a bawdy-house – that must be an act of purest sarcasm, surely? Nobody could be so innocent.

Unsteady on her feet (for she had wine last night),

Sugar shambles to the window and looks down into the alley from her top-floor vantage-point. Her tormentor is a fat matron in a black bonnet, accompanied by a miserable-looking child toting a basketful of pamphlets: two dark blots on the brightly-lit cobbles.

> *Set thy sights on Heaven's gleaming,*
> *Look about thee for employ;*
> *Linger not in idle dreaming;*
> *Labour is the sweetest joy!*

Sugar shivers where she stands. It's spring, but not exactly warm. In fact, despite the brilliant sunshine, there's a wintry nip in the air. She's slept in her clothes all night, and her sweat is now cooling, making her feel as though she's stepped out of a bath and wrapped herself in an unpleasantly damp towel. She hugs herself and rubs her thin arms vigorously with her palms.

The missionary in the street below, sensing movement above her head, glances upwards, but Sugar steps back at once. She'll display every detail of her naked body to her customers, but she won't allow passersby to ogle her outside of working hours. Let them pay if they want a look.

The do-gooder sings louder, sniffing an audience; her voice almost cracks with the force of her delivery, as she flings a new song at Mrs Castaway's top storey.

*Have I long in sin been sleeping,*
*O, forgive and rescue me!*
*Lord! I crave Your showers of blessing*
*Let Your mercy fall on me!*

Fall on me? Sugar momentarily considers pulling on a glove, fishing a turd out of her chamber-pot and throwing it down onto the head of this caterwauling ninny – *there's* God's mercy for you! But she'd probably miss, and ruin a glove for nothing. And there's no guarantee the singing would stop, anyway; these Christian crusaders can be as tenacious as a dog in heat. Better to lose herself in an activity of her own.

She gets back into bed, still fully dressed, and wraps the bedsheet around her bony shoulders like a shawl. Yawns like a cat. For the duration of the yawn, the sound of the evangelist is suppressed, lost in the bloodstream commotion inside her ears. If she could only yawn for half an hour on end, the woman outside her window would surely hoarsen and go home.

Next to Sugar's bed is a stack of books and periodicals. Trollope's *He Knew He Was Right*, collected in
book form, is topmost, but she won't read any more
of that: she can see where it's heading. It wasn't so
bad at the start, but now he's put a strong-minded
woman into it, whom he clearly detests, so he'll probably humiliate or kill her before the story's finished.
And she's fed up with Trollope's latest serial, *The Way
We Live Now* – she won't buy any more instalments,
it's threatening to go on forever, and she's wasted
enough money on it already. Really, she doesn't know
why she persists with Trollope; he may be refresh-
ingly unsentimental, but he always pretends he's on
the woman's side, then lets the men win. They all do,
these novelists, whether they're male or female: the
game is rigged. And the latest Mrs Riddell is worse
than usual, and there hasn't been a tolerable serial in
*The London Journal* for months, only garbage about
ghosts and forged wills. In every story she reads, the
women are limp and spineless and insufferably vir-
tuous. They harbour no hatred, they think only of
marriage, they don't exist below the neck, they eat
but never shit. Where are the authentic, flesh-and-
blood women in modern English fiction? There aren't
any!

She turns her face away from the stack of books and periodicals. She was foolish to buy them in the first place. (Well, granted, a few of them she stole.) What is the point of reading other people's stories? She ought to be writing her own. Reading, by its very nature, is an admission of defeat, a ritual of self-humiliation: it shows that you believe other lives are more interesting than yours. Sugar suddenly wishes she could scrape her soul clean of all the fictional heroines she has ever cared about, claim back all the hours she has wasted worrying about star-crossed lovers and tragic misunderstandings. All of it is trickery, a Punch and Judy show for the gullible masses. Who will write the truth if she doesn't write it herself? Nobody.

*And will the portals open,* yammers the evangelist,
*To me who roamed so long*
*Filthy, and vile and burdened*
*With this great weight of wrong . . .*

Sugar considers hurrying downstairs and opening the portals of Mrs Castaway's brothel to this idiot. Why not drag her indoors? Introduce her to the smell of semen? Offer her a swig of gin? A generous dose of Christian hospitality.

She edges back up to the window, peers down at the evangelist, who has paused in her song and stands still, head bent, as if in prayer. In truth, she is bending down to listen to her child. Her child is saying something Sugar cannot hear. The mother hunches down lower, visibly annoyed that the child's words make no sense to her. The child begins to whimper and sniffle, evidently fed up with standing in the glare and the chill, singing to nobody in an alleyway that smells of fermenting horse piss.

After several seconds of flustered communication, the mother rummages in her basket and, from under the religious pamphlets, extracts an apple. She offers it to the child, who begins to weep louder. The mother seizes the little girl's hand and pushes the apple into it, but the child's grip fumbles – accidentally? wilfully? – and the fruit falls to the ground. At once – as though the impact of the apple has released a tripwire attached to the mother's arm – the mother slaps the child in the face. The child, poorly balanced, trips and falls.

Sugar is on the stairs before she has time to think. She's barefoot, clad in a bodice and rumpled skirt but without bonnet or shawl: barely dressed, in other words. She leaps down the stairs two steps at a time, determined to assault the evangelist, smash her ugly nose, crush her windpipe, break her skull on the cobbles like an over-ripe melon.

She bursts out of Mrs Castaway's and out onto the street. The evangelist and the child are gone.

Sugar makes a noise like a cornered cat. She lurches first in one direction, then another, then teeters around. They can't have vanished so soon! She hurries from the deserted mews to Silver Street proper, and peers up and down the thoroughfare. There's a fruit barrow with Fat Meg behind it, and Fat Meg's dog, scratching himself in the sun. There's an old man selling shirt collars on a stick. A street-sweeper waiting for horse-turds to fall. Tess, a prostitute from a rival house, struggling to open a stiff parasol. Two swells, striding purposefully towards a cab they've hailed. A group of hard-faced, grubby boys in cloth caps. A policeman, watchful for illegal behaviours that have not been rendered invisible by bribery. But no fat matron in a black bonnet, no little girl.

Sugar stands in the public street, aware all of a sudden that she is barefoot, that the soles of her naked feet are pressed against gritty, probably shit-soiled cobbles; aware that her unbrushed hair is being lifted by the breeze, and that her bodice is unhooked at the back, and that everyone can see. Her legs are trembling with rage and frustration, but they might as well be trembling because she's just been fucked against a wall. Tess, the rival whore, snaps her parasol open at last and, raising it, notices Sugar at last. Their eyes meet across a distance of fifty yards or so. Sugar turns sharply – cutting her left heel on a jagged stone – and flees.

Back in her bedroom at Mrs Castaway's bawdy-house, Sugar soaks her feet in a washtub. The injury is nothing to speak of. The dirt is floating free already. It was plain, nondescript dirt, street grime, not shit; for this she is grateful. Soon she will dry her feet and rub them with scented oil.

Her heart has stopped thumping now. It beats inside her breast, regular and only a little harder than usual. She is master – or is it mistress? – of herself again. How to account for her lapse? How could she have acted so foolishly, when she prides herself on her cool judgement? A man can insult her in the vilest conceivable manner, and she can continue her business with a calm face and an icy heart. It is a point of honour with her that none of her customers has

ever had the faintest idea what she was truly feeling.
Yet this morning she has chased after a stranger, helpless with fury. She stood dishevelled and confused in
public, her distress evident to any passerby. This
must never happen again.

Still soaking her feet in the tub, she reaches over
to the stack of reading matter and seizes hold of
the topmost thing. It's an issue of *Purefoy's Home &
Family Companion*, which she buys avidly despite
having no real home, no family and no companion.
She buys it because it includes a monthly summary
of all the important things that have happened in
the world, explained in simplified terms that ignorant young ladies and dim-witted matrons can
understand. Sugar, who despises the pompous
intrigues of politicians and the vain-glorious
exploits of businessmen, would be happy to remain
perfectly ignorant of everything that goes on outside Soho, but she's found that a rudimentary grasp
of current affairs can be useful in her line of work:
she can learn just enough to feign agreement with
the views of her clients. And *Purefoy's Home & Family
Companion* has other things in it as well: pictures of
pretty clothes, engravings of exotic animals from
all over the Empire, advertisements, testimonials —

and a serialised novel. It's to this that Sugar turns
as she soaks her feet.

*Chapter 13: UNMASKED!*

*Oh, the predicament of poor Hornsby as he led
the innocent Fred into foul streets the like of which
the lad had plainly never seen before. On the one
hand, he had a solemn duty, as Fred's best friend,
to pull him back from the precipitous decision to
which he, Fred, was, in his lamentable ignorance, so
unswervingly committed. On the other hand,
Hornsby knew that the grief his friend would, in
the minutes that were to follow, experience, would be
of such dreadful intensity that this noble young man
might never — not if he lived to be a hundred —
recover from it.*

*'There must be some mistake,' said Fred, noting
with growing alarm the shabby character of the
dwellings they were passing, and the brute depravity
on the faces of the inhabitants. 'My lovely Violet
cannot possibly live here.'*

*Hornsby made no reply, but pulled his friend ever
deeper into the cesspool of wickedness.*

*'This is the house,' he said at last, as they came
to a halt in front of the shabbiest, meanest house of*

*them all; a house whose walls, were they not black-ened with grime, might have blushed in cognizance of the depraved exploits transacted within them.*

*'It cannot be,' weakly remonstrated the ghastly-pale lad.*

*'If, by cutting off my right arm at the shoulder, I could unmake the truth of it, I beg you to believe I would do so, my friend,' said Hornsby. 'But this wretched abode, it pains me infinitely to say, is the home of that false creature to whom you are engaged.'*

*The unhappy lad, profoundly offended by this slur upon the virtue of the person he loved more than any other, turned exceedingly red in the cheeks, and gathered his soft white hands into fists, poised to strike at his friend. But at that instant, the door of the sordid house in front of which they stood flew open, and there, in its dark, dismal, worm-eaten doorway, tainted by unwholesome shadows, stood Violet, aghast. Aghast for a moment only! — before she imposed upon her countenance a look of delighted surprise.*

*'Beloved!' she cried. 'You never told me you were in the habit of performing charitable works! And what an extraordinary coincidence that our ministering pur-poses should cross in this most pitiful of places! I have*

*just finished delivering to the wretched folk here a parcel of clean clothing, some soap and a pamphlet of Bible verses.*

What the mortified Fred said in response to this unlikely declaration, Sugar doesn't wait to find out. In a blind fury, she rips *Purefoy's Home & Family Companion* into shreds, flinging it piecemeal all over her bedroom.

Once again, she's out of breath, panting like a dog. Once again, her heart is beating far too loud against her rib-cage. Once again, damn it, she has allowed herself to lose her grip. She'll never get out of Silver Street if she carries on like this. Only the steeliest resolve and the chilliest heart will rescue her from a life of subjection. A moment will come, on a day unheralded by any forewarning, when she will be presented with an opportunity to escape her fate, and she must be ready for that moment. A powerful man will stray into her life, with the intention of using her once and then disappearing back to his exalted sphere. But in the heat of the moment, he will let slip a confession, or mention a name he'd intended to keep secret, or perhaps he will simply get a look in his eye that she can match with her own, and there he'll be: caught. It could happen in any of a hundred ways, ways she can't even imagine on this humdrum morning in her hatefully familiar room with its faded wallpaper and rotten skirting-boards and rumpled old bedclothes. The only certain thing is that this golden opportunity will come once only, and her mind will need to be unclouded, her emotions strapped down.

She notices a pain in her right fist. Uncurling her fingers, she winces as a hair-thin slit opens up in the tender flesh between her palm and her middle finger. A paper cut. She has injured herself on *Purefoy's Home & Family Companion*. Another lesson in restraint.

Sugar removes her feet from the tub and dries them on the hem of her petticoats. The skin on her soles has gone pale and wrinkled; tiny pellets of flesh rub off. The scratch on her heel is bloodless now. It has stopped hurting, although the paper cut on her hand is exquisitely bothersome.

It's high time she got properly dressed and groomed. She walks over to the window, combing her hair. She looks down into the mews, at the cobbles. There's nobody there now. But, balanced on her windowsill, ready, is the apple, shiny and firm. Sugar snatched it up from the ground as she stumbled back to the house, loath to let it be scavenged by dogs, and now here it sits, scarcely bruised. Maybe the evangelist will return this afternoon, or tomorrow, or the day after tomorrow; the apple will keep for a while. And, if the evangelist should return, Sugar will take the apple in hand, aim with the utmost care, and throw – straight and true.

*Medicine*

illiam Rackham sits at his desk and examines the label of the medicine he is about to take. He hopes there's no morphine or cocaine in these little yellow pills, because the swig of Rennick's Restorative Syrup he swallowed just an hour ago was generously laced with narcotics, and he still feels rather peculiar. Each passing year makes him less tolerant of intoxicants; he would gladly do without them altogether, were he not so prone to all sorts of complaints.

'*Persons of A FULL HABIT, who are subject to Headache, Depression of Spirits, Dullness of Sight, Nervous Affections, Singing in the Ears, Spasms, and all Disorders of the Stomach and Bowels, should never be without Frampton's Pills of Health*', says the label on the bottle. The ingredients aren't specified, however, except for the routine assurance that they are entirely natural, pure and unadulterated. William Rackham shakes one pill into his wrinkled palm and lifts it close to his nose. His long experience as a perfumer would certainly allow him to identify the smell of opium if any were perceptible. There is none.

He lays his hand down on the desktop, fingers folded loosely over the pill, delaying the moment. There is always the hope that he will draw a deep breath, exhale slowly, and feel the illness drain out of his body in an unexpected, delirious thrill. He draws the breath, exhales, waits. A gust of wind rattles his study window, and the lamplight dims momentarily, making him feel as though the walls of his room are contracting. He knows every inch of these walls, every calcifying spine of every long-unread book in the bookcases, every glint on the burnished wood of the clock, every yellowish blemish on the clockface, every faded print in every outmoded frame, every hairline crack in the ceiling cornices, every tiny air-bubble trapped behind the wallpaper. It seems like months since he set foot outside this gloomy sanctum.

It's high time he paid a visit to his lavender fields. The journey to Surrey would be a tonic in itself; just to get away from London and its air of suffocating competition, its pervading sense of a million human creatures jostling and gasping for their own lungful of life. How sweet it would be to walk in the fresh air, with the sun overhead and damp soil underfoot, and the smell of acres of lovingly-tended lavender in his nose.

A cold chill runs down his back, as though a prankster is trickling ice-water under his shirt-collar. An intolerable itch attacks the insides of his nostrils and, before he can fetch his handkerchief from his pocket, he sneezes mightily. A hundred specks of opaque, watery snot are sprayed all over his desk. They glimmer on the surface of the dark green leather inlay.

William Rackham stares at the vista in dismay. If he summons a servant to clean up the mess, she will take one look at his desk, and another at his guilty face, and judge him to be no better than a helpless infant. But surely a man of his standing should not be cleaning up snot? And what should he use to clean it if he did? His handkerchief is white silk, and his desk is stained with ink, mottled with dusting-powder and, to be quite frank, a little mildewy on parts of the leather surface. His sleeve . . . Almighty God, is this a fair fate for a man who has already suffered a thousand humiliations? Wiping up snot with his sleeve?

He bends in his creaky chair and, with his free

hand, retrieves a couple of crumpled sheets of paper from the wicker waste-basket. If he wields them with care, they will serve as cleaning-rags. Best possible use for them, really, these letters from people who no longer welcome the overtures of William Rackham, Esq.

Two sheets of crumpled paper. His correspondence has dwindled remarkably in the last decade and a half, dwindled along with his empire. 'Empire'? Too grand a word, he knows. It never quite applied to Rackham Perfumeries, did it? But what word to use instead? 'Business' sounds grubby. 'Concern', that's the safest. His dwindling concern.

Ah, but who could have blamed him for using the word 'empire', in those heady years when the world lay before him? Who could have failed to be swept up in his own pride, when he first mounted the crest of Beehive Hill, and looked down upon the vast rolling fields of lavender, the shimmering lake of *Lavandula*, his industrious domain? It seemed inconceivable that his manufactures should not make their way into every shop in the country – and for a brief time, in the mid-1870s, it was almost so. Nowadays, Newcastle, Leeds and Glasgow are still strongholds of his merchandise, and, for some reason that he's never fully understood, regular shipments go to Calcutta. But here at home . . . He uncrumples a letter from a household goods emporium in Walthamstow, whose manager points out that the toiletries shelves are already overflowing with other men's soaps and bathwaters. William sweeps the hateful piece of paper back and forth across his desktop, mopping the specks of snot with it. A second letter – unsolicited mail from the Tariff Reform League – scuffs the leather dry. All is well, until the next sneeze.

William tosses one of Frampton's Pills of Health into his mouth and washes it down with a gulp of port. Alcohol is the best thing, really, for colds; better than any number of quack remedies and expensive drugs. Were it not for the absolute necessity of remaining sober enough to do his work, he would polish off a few bottles of port and wake up a day or two later, cured.

He picks up his pen, loads it with ink, and begins to write. Scratch, scratch, scratch. Determination is all. There is no time for self-pity. Push ahead, ignoring one's suffering, and before one knows it the job is done.

Minutes later, a knock on his study door. It's

Letty, the maid, bringing him a plate of bread and cold meats.

'The luncheon you asked for, Mr Rackham,' she says.

He cannot recall asking for this. It does look like the sort of thing he would ask for, though, if he were peckish, which he suddenly remembers he is.

'Thank you, Letty,' he says.

She carries her serving-tray to his desk, puts the plate on the old brown ledger-book according to long-established custom.

'Cup of tea, Mr Rackham?'

'No thank you, Letty, I have a fever.'

'Oh, I'm sorry to hear that, Mr Rackham. Coffee?'

The half-empty bottle of port is standing on the desk, in plain view. William appraises the servant's face, finds it vaguely well-disposed and unjudgemental, as always.

'Yes, some coffee,' he says. And, with a nod that is half-way to a curtsey, the servant backs out of the room.

Good old Letty. He likes her. She's not pretty anymore, and she's grown rather scrawny and wrinkled, and walks with an unladylike gait, the result of crumbling hip-bones. But a servant shouldn't be ladylike anyway; Rose was like that, with airs above her station. She left him in the lurch after only a few years of service, poached by a richer man. Letty is loyal, God bless her. And who'd have her now, if she weren't? She's lucky to have an indulgent master. He will keep her until she drops.

William lays aside his correspondence and selects a slice of meat. Roast beef, from yesterday's dinner. Still succulent, with a nice crisp rind and a pink blush in the middle. His latest cook is not at all bad, despite her lack of talent for desserts. Lord, how many cooks has he had in the last fifteen years? It must be half a dozen. Why can't these women remain in a good position when they're put in one?

'This is an unhappy house, Mr Rackham,' one of the departing cooks told him. Stupid pug-faced biddy: she did precious little to make it happier! Her breakfast toast always had an ashy texture, and her puddings never had enough sugar in them. He would probably have dismissed her, if she hadn't left first, and if it hadn't been such an inconvenience to lose her.

The thought of puddings makes William crave something sweet. His luncheon plate is all savoury:

roast beef, silverside, smoked ham. Even the butter on the bread is generously salted. Could he call Letty back and ask her to fetch him some marmalade? Or better still, some cake and custard? Or even better yet, some hot apple crumble, dusted all over with sugar?

*Anything you ask of me.* That's what she said. That's how she snared him. Sugar. The whore who called herself Sugar. Promised him all his dreams fulfilled. As whores always do.

No day goes by when he doesn't think of her. He had hundreds before her, and he's had a few since, but she was the one who wrote herself into his heart – and then stabbed it with the pen, god damn her.

He leans his head back wearily, eyes shut. The vision of Sugar that looms in the darkness ought to be a lurid spectre, a cloaked phantom with a skeleton head, as befits those creatures who lure upright men into alleyways and taint them with disease. But instead, he recalls a brilliant April afternoon in his lavender fields, when Sugar walked at his side, looking as fresh and lovely as the sunlit blooms all around. Her gloves and bonnet were so white he could scarcely look at them. Her face was in shade, gaze downcast, except when he urged her to look at something. Then her eyes were shiny with awe; the wonders he was showing her were too much to take in. He felt as if he owned the whole world, the sky above, and, most keenly of all, this exquisite girl with her long pale neck and her ochre curls haloed with gold.

Of course she was false to the bone. How could he have failed to guess that? A hard-up whore and a successful businessman – the arithmetic of it is too obvious for words. Before he met her, he was a healthy fellow, strong and upright. And then . . . ? It's difficult, looking back, to see precisely how she made the fabric of his life unravel, what strings she pulled. But the evidence is overwhelming: within a year of becoming ensnared in her wiles, he was a stuttering invalid, and his family was utterly destroyed.

Oh, Agnes! Oh, his poor little wife! He let himself be distracted, and she perished for lack of his nurture. Sickly thing that she was, she might yet have thrived; there were signs she was improving. Who's to say he might not have rescued her, had he not been bamboozled by Sugar's constant whisperings in his ear? How can he ever forgive himself for allowing a viper into his home, installing her in his household, entrusting his daughter into her care? And who's to say Sugar didn't exert her poisonous influence over Agnes too, to fatal effect? Everything she ever did had one purpose only: to make herself the next Mrs Rackham. But damn her, there could only ever be one Mrs Rackham, and that was his dear little Agnes!

'Excuse me, Mr Rackham,' says Letty, suddenly standing in front of him with a cup of coffee. 'Mrs Rackham wants to know if you need the doctor.'

'Mrs Rackham?' he echoes. 'Doctor?' He has momentary difficulty summoning a mental picture of either of these persons. Then he recalls old Doctor Curlew, white-haired and cadaverous. The image of Mrs Rackham comes a moment later.

'Tell her I'm improving.'

'Yes, Mr Rackham.'

'What's she doing today?'

'Receiving a visit from Mr St John, Mr Rackham.'

'He was here yesterday, too.'

'Yes, Mr Rackham.'

He nods to dismiss her. It's important that she knows he has a grip on what's happening in his own house.

Alone with his coffee, William reflects on his re-marriage. Constance has been a benign, unobtrusive presence in his life. Of all the many disappointments he's had to swallow during the last fifteen years, Constance has been among the smallest. In the grievous aftermath of losing his family, she offered him another, and he was relieved of the pain of being pitied: 'That's William Rackham, poor wretch: his wife walked into the Thames.' Constance did her very best to write a new chapter of the Rackham family history; she wears his name proudly in public. Only . . . She never did give him the heir she hinted she might, and now she is past the age for such things, and they scarcely see each other. He labours in his study; she socialises. He cannot picture any part of her below the chin.

Sugar had sharp hips, such sharp hips. You felt them digging into your abdomen as you moved inside. The palms of her hands were rough-textured: some sort of skin ailment. Odd that he never feared catching pox from her. God knows what depravities she indulged in before he discovered her; she had a reputation for doing what other girls refused.

*Anything you ask of me.*

How warm her body was, how accommodating! How divine it was, to slide his prick into her silky cunt! And more than this, how divine to know that her answer to his every question was Yes, Yes, Yes.

Not in a mindless, obedient fashion, like a servant; more like . . . a friend.

Once again, he returns, in his memory, to the afternoon in the lavender field. There is something about that day which resists bitter reappraisal; all the dark muck of betrayal, the oily filth of cynicism, can be emptied over it and nothing sticks; the day is left clean and fresh-smelling. How is it possible, after all that's happened? Yet here he goes again, stepping back into the April of 1875, standing once more together with Sugar on the crest of Beehive Hill. They're facing north-east: there's a swathe of rain far, far away, sprouting a rainbow. William stares at his mistress from behind, his hand shielding his eyes against the sun. Sugar's long skirts rustle in the breeze, her shoulderblades poke through the tight fabric of her dress as she lifts her arm to shield her face. The wind rises; the lavender stirs gently below as though he and Sugar were on the prow of a boat adrift on a lilac sea.

What is she looking at? The same thing he is looking at. And what is that? Everything and nothing. There is a kind of fear in her eyes; a recognition that there is too much beauty here, that the universe is too big and humans too small. With a few words, if he speaks now, he can restore the balance. With a few words, if he can only find them in time . . . But then Sugar raises her arm higher still, and shifts the inclination of her hips, and her dress clings to her body differently from how it clung a moment before, and he sees the slight swell of her bosom through the fabric, and he recalls how those breasts feel against his palms. Abruptly he aches to strip her naked, to push her down on her hands and knees, to spread the cheeks of her arse until her cunt yawns open . . .

*Anything you ask of me.*

He forces his eyes open. It is wrong for a man past his middle years to reminisce tenderly about a whore. He is a respectable man, not some dissolute bohemian. The idle friends of his youth are long gone, unfit companions for a man of his standing. He is a pillar of the community, a pillar. His hand is down his trousers, massaging his erection, or pushing it down, he's not sure which. How hungry she was for him! – if what she said could be believed. And no woman can be believed. The world is a sticky mess of betrayal.

Agnes. If he has amorous thoughts, they ought to be about her. She was his flower, his little treasure.

She was innocent and unpolluted. No man had laid a hand on her naked flesh until he came. She lay beside him, under him, stiff and clammy, like a chilled ham carved into the shape of a woman. He should never have touched her. Why did he touch her? Because she was the most delicious little thing, and he had earned the right to have her. A man is not a saint.

He leans his head back against the top of his chair. Digs the hard wood into his scalp, to combat the throbbing in his brain. Today can still be a productive day, if he can get his fever under control. The medicine should begin to take effect any minute now.

Oh, what a pretty girl she was. Pretty as a blossom, and as pale. Spoiled blossoms, the mortuary slab. The machines in his factory in Surrey; God damn the man who sold them to him. A fortune's-worth of lavender petals, all spoiled, tainted with engine oil, suffused with the ineradicable smell of burning. Nothing to be done but wait for the next harvest. At the mercy of Nature and his competitors. Lord save him: no one else will. Sugar's lips: how dry they were, how feathery against his own. How satisfying she was to kiss. But he has no business thinking of her, no business. That afternoon in April is a mirage; it never was; it is a pretty illusion shimmering over a clump of ordure.

The corpse on the mortuary slab. Men had forced him to look at a body half eaten away by fish. The face was a skull. He had said it was Agnes. Was it Agnes? He looks again. The face fleshes out a little, then a little more, teasingly taking on human form in increments of skin. He stares, transfixed. Like a candle magically unmelting itself, the woman's flesh is restored on the bone, until Agnes's eyes, cheeks and mouth are clearly recognisable. Yes, yes, he should never have doubted. The ambience of the mortuary loses its harshness, and before long, the trolley on which Agnes lies is more like a bed, and she wears a white gown like a nun or an angel, faintly glowing in gentle light.

Now happy memories of his lost little wife take hold of him. He recalls the enchanting, peculiar lass she was when they first met, a sweetly scented stranger. She was seventeen, but looked younger. She held herself as though she'd developed a bosom only yesterday or the day before, and hadn't a clue what to do with it. If she was aware of being watched, she could walk with gracious poise, but if she forgot herself, she would skip along in a flurry of skirts, and if she was tickled by some remark or occurrence, she would giggle infectiously like a child. Seated in the right sort of chair in the right sort of setting, however, she resembled a portrait of a lady by Sir Joshua Reynolds. She could certainly act as demurely as any duchess who ever hid her smile behind a fan. She wore only bright colours, and favoured white, so that in the noonday sunlight she shone so brilliantly that he must cup his hand over his brow.

*Go play with someone else. You are hurting me.*

He butts his head against the chair-back, groaning. Fate is cruel, fate is vicious. All one's overtures of love are rejected, all one's well-meaning is misunderstood, all one's business plans come to nought. No, No, and No – *that* is Fate's answer. Even the chance to have a son and see the next generation reaping fruit where one's own labours were unrewarded: Fate said No. Who will inherit his empire? 'Empire'? Well, whatever it is, who will inherit it? Constance. She who meets him daily for dinner as though they were both guests in a hotel, conversing politely, their eyes slightly glazed as they stare into the invisible horizons of their separate lives. What

Constance knows about toiletry manufacture would fit on the head of a pin. She will bury him, shed a few tears, feed his business into the mouth of one of the bigger fish, and move on. Good old Constance, patient Constance, forbearing Constance. Waiting all these years while he sits at his desk, scribbling himself sum by sum into his coffin.

Somewhere, though, he has a child. His sole issue. God alone knows where she is; the police certainly don't. Sophie. He named her Sophie. She might have been the delight of his old age. She might have given him a grandson to pass the business onto. She might, for all he knows, be working in a brothel, servicing drunken louts while Sugar sits counting the money. She might, for all he knows, be dead.

Anguish blurs his vision as he tries to imagine his daughter as an adult. Instead, he sees only a crimson, swollen child's face streaming with tears, and hears Sophie's whining voice pleading not to be separated from her beloved Miss Sugar. Oh, the poisonous cleverness of that woman, to have bewitched his daughter just as she bewitched him! 'Stop that now, Sophie,' he commanded her, but she was unable to obey. 'Open your pretty blue eyes and look at me,' he commanded, but she defied him.

Blue eyes. Yes, she had blue eyes. Pretty blue eyes indeed. Like her mother. 'She has your eyes' – that's what he told Agnes, directly after the birth, when the midwife had hustled the baby out of the room and Agnes lay delirious in her bloody bed. It was the most encouraging thing he could think of to say, given the severity of his disappointment in the sex of his child. 'She has your eyes.'

'No!' Agnes screamed, hiding her face behind her hands as though he were attempting to dig her eye-balls out of their sockets with a spoon. 'No one has my eyes! No one but me!'

Mimicking his wife's self-protective motion, William jerks his hands up to his face, which is cold and damp. In doing so, he knocks over the port bottle. Fortunately it's empty, although he can't recall drinking the rest. It rolls off his desk onto the floor, landing with a musical clunk. He bends down in his chair to retrieve it.

In the dizzy swirl of darkness that follows, he tumbles freely. It is not at all like falling off a chair onto the floor. It is like being an umbrella snatched up by a gust of wind, or a top hat blown off a man's head, spinning through the air, beyond reach, to land God knows where. Will someone catch him?

*You poor baby.*

A female voice. He is on his back. He is no longer falling. The darkness has given way to a pulsating red, and he lies in an underground subway, or perhaps a sewer, staring up at the vaulted brickwork. Each brick glows as though heated in a forge. Sweat prickles up through his pores; trapped warmth seems to swell inside his skin, threatening to burst out.

Suddenly hovering over him is a young whore with dark hair and a powdered face. Her eyes gleam with murderous delight. He tries to crawl away, but many hands seize hold of his clothing and begin to rip him naked. Only when they are finished with him do they allow him to slither away on a slick of filthy water and his own blood.

*Help me*, he mouths, for he has lost the power of speech.

*I'm here, William.*

Sugar's voice. He recognises it at once, even after fifteen years without it. Warm, sincere, slightly hoarse. The most beguiling voice in the world.

'Leave me in peace,' he groans.

*Let me help you.*

'You've helped me enough,' he retorts, shutting

his eyes tight. 'My dear Agnes is dead. You've taken my daughter from me. I am old before my time.'

*Shhhhhhhh* . . .

He feels her hand on his face. Her palm is as rough as ever, rough as bark. She strokes his cheek with breathtaking tenderness. He hasn't felt a touch so tender in the five and a half thousand days since she left him. If he opens his eyes, he knows he'll see her, and that he will weep with joy at seeing her, and that he will confess that he has lost his way, that he has been wandering all these years like an abandoned child in a dark forest, longing for her to find him and take him home. He senses she's bending down to kiss him; the soft curls of her abundant hair fall against his neck and shoulders; her breath dampens his lips.

'Mr Rackham?'

He struggles weakly against her embrace (what kind of fool does she think he is?), while at the same time he yearns to be enfolded in her arms, to wail into her bosom, to disappear between her legs.

'Mr Rackham?'

Her gentle touch on his cheek becomes a pat, then a hesitant slap. He opens his eyes. There are two women squatting over his body, each seizing him under an armpit and attempting to heave him up off the carpet. Their faces swim into focus. One face is Letty's. The other – better-preserved, bright-eyed, sharp-nosed – is his wife's.

'I'm all right,' he croaks. 'Leave me.'

'You're awful hot, Mr Rackham,' says Letty.

'Burning up, I'd say,' says Constance, laying a hand on his forehead, unfussily, as though assessing the warmth of a teapot.

'I have a fever,' he concedes. 'It'll pass.'

'Doctor Curlew is on his way,' says Constance.

'No, no,' he mutters, as they help him back onto his chair. 'No.'

'It's done, William.'

He groans again, this time in annoyance. He cannot afford to lose more time than he has already lost. Rackham Toiletries is under siege from competitors. Its territory must be defended.

'Leave me, leave me,' he implores.

The two women glance at each other. He is not so feverish that he fails to notice them sharing a glimmer of illicit intimacy. Women against men. So profound and universal is this female antagonism that it can even cross the gulf between mistress and servant. He knows, oh yes he knows.

'Leave me.'

The two women do as he asks. Letty can hardly disobey, can she? As for Constance, dear sweet Constance, dear patient Constance, she gives him one of her mildly hurt looks. She'll cheer up, no doubt, as soon as she steps out into her congenial playground of social intercourse. She'll drink her tea, her little finger raised, her sparkling eyes focused on whomever has dropped in on her today, while her husband toils un-noticed behind one of the many closed doors upstairs.

William sits straight in his chair, squares his shoulders, smooths his thinning hair flat to his scalp. He took a little too much medicine; that's plain. Lucidity has returned. He still has a fever, but it won't stop him doing what has to be done. A cold chill runs down his back, as though a prankster is trickling ice-water under his shirt-collar. An intolerable itch attacks the insides of his nostrils . . . but this time it doesn't catch him napping. Quick as thought, he fetches his handkerchief from his pocket and sneezes mightily into it. Not a drop spilled.

He breathes deeply. The day is still young. He examines the contents of his desk. A cup of cold coffee. The pile of unanswered correspondence. His inkwell and pen. He retrieves the letter he'd been writing, ready to resume where he'd left off. A quarter of the page has already been filled, in his somewhat untidy script.

He cracks his fingers, takes up the pen, slides the page into position, and reviews what it says so far.

*Begin,* is all it says. *Begin begin begin begin begin . . .*

*A Mighty Horde of Women
in Very Big Hats, Advancing*

**M**y father made half of me. Exactly half, my mother said. She didn't specify which half, so for some time I imagined my head, arms and chest to be the handiwork of my father, who was the artistic type and might therefore have enjoyed the challenge of crafting my facial features – especially my eyes, which seemed to me miraculous bits of apparatus. As for my mother, I imagined her taking responsibility for my lower torso, legs and genitals. (There was nothing sexual in this, I hasten to add: I was only seven, and you must remember that it was a different era.)

My misunderstanding about the manufacture of children might have become one of those beliefs that we can never quite unbelieve, one of those daft convictions whose last chance to be removed is overlooked one Tuesday morning in April and which consequently burrows deep into our brain. But it was not destined for that. My mother and I were very intimate, you see. We had long conversations each day, about everything. I suppose I must have made some remark about the half of me my father had made, perhaps speculating about the authorship of my belly-button, because I remember her giving me a corrective lecture about *ingredients*. Each human person was a mixture of ingredients, like a soup, she said. The mother provided half of them and the father the other half. Then they all got mixed up and cooked and the result was the child, in this case me.

To be honest, I rather preferred the mistaken version of the story. I didn't like to think of myself as a bag of stew, an envelope of pale skin with all sorts of dark, gooey stuff slopping around inside. It was undignified, not to mention alarming. I was an adventurous boy, and had spent my first six years in the wilds of Australia, crawling over stony terrain, falling off logs, rolling around in dirt, and generally taking advantage of my permissive familial circumstances. I knew all about scratches and bruises, but the thought that a chance injury might spill out my entire contents: that was something else.

Looking back now, I can see that the spring of 1908 was not an innocent season like the ones before it, but a conspiracy of alarms, a concerted assault on my childish self-confidence. The news about my soupy ingredients was just one of many intrusions into what had been, until then, a life of serenely self-absorbed play. I suppose the time had come for me to learn that I was not exempt from History, but mixed up in it.

You know, because I was a child in what's now called the Edwardian era, and because I was born the day Queen Victoria died, I always think of the Edwardians as children. Children who lost their mother, but were too young to realise she was gone, and therefore played on just as before, only gradually noticing, out of the corners of their eyes, the flickering shadows outside their sunny nursery. Shadows of commotion, of unrest. Sounds of argument, of protest, of Mother's things being tossed into boxes, of fixtures being forcibly unscrewed, of the whole house being dismantled. And the child plays nervously on, humming a familiar little tune.

Was I aware that the English empire was under siege from its own subjects? Was I aware that, while I was fashioning warrior spears out of gum tree twigs in the semi-savage suburbia of the Great Southern Land, all sorts of troublemakers had been rising up in London, like the Labour Party, the suffragettes, Sinn Fein, the Indian Home Rule Society, and trade unions of every stamp? Was I aware that there were strikes, hunger marches, pickets, riots? Of course I wasn't. Even prime ministers behaved as if none of this was happening. But eventually, the removal men cannot wait any longer; they barge into the nursery, and start ripping the pretty pictures from the walls, and the child covers its eyes, but can't help peeping through them. That's what was happening in 1908.

The first things I noticed were strictly personal, of course. For some reason I never understood, my family had decided to return 'home'. Home for me had always been Australia, so the thought that we had somehow been lost or only on holiday, and must travel twelve thousand miles on a ship to find our proper beds, was shocking. But my mother insisted that home was England, and six weeks of seaborne misery later, that's where we were. Our new abode was in Calthorpe Street, Bloomsbury, which my mother told me was not very far from where the great Charles Dickens had once lived. I hadn't a clue who this person was; all I knew was that I was now very, very far from where *I* had once lived.

To add to my confusion, my first day at school made me doubt the new home address I had memorised so carefully. A sour-faced old lady wrote my name in a ledger and informed me, in a voice dripping with disdain, that Calthorpe Street was not in Bloomsbury but in Clerkenwell. My parents denied this so insistently that I began to think they must be in the wrong, and to this day I hesitate for a moment before claiming that I ever lived in Bloomsbury, even though I've since been assured by many experts that Calthorpe Street is most definitely not in Clerkenwell and that the sour-faced old lady was the one at fault. But that's Britain for you. Within minutes of setting foot inside my new school, I'd learned how much unease can be generated out of bloody nothing.

And what an education I got! For the first time, I had English playmates, rather than a rabble of Antipodeans adrift from the confines of class and decorum. It seemed incredible that children so young should have such a sophisticated and comprehensive knowledge of social subtleties. But they did. Everything, from one's street address to the positioning of a coat-button, was loaded with meaning, and the meaning was usually a humiliation.

One's parents, of course, were one's Achilles heel. One was made to feel that one had chosen them, and chosen badly. In learning what English children considered normal, I got the message that almost everything about my parents was abnormal. At Torrington Infants School, judgement was passed according to an intangible textbook of rules, and my parents were guilty of infringements galore. For instance: my mother had given birth to me, her first child, in her early thirties; this was most bizarre, even Biblically far-fetched. In fact, according to some of my schoolmates, it was simply impossible. Surely she must have been married before, and left behind a brood of strapping children, in order to begin afresh with a new man? I summoned up the courage to ask Mama if Papa was her first husband.

'Of course he is,' she said with a grin. 'And he'll be the last, I promise you.'

'But what were you doing before?'

'Exploring the world.'

'Like explorers in Africa?'

'Exactly like explorers in Africa. Except not in Africa.'

'Where, then?'

'I've told you where, many times.'

'But why weren't you married?'

She peered into the distance, as if trying to spot a landmark lost in mist.

'I wasn't ready.'

'All other women get married when they're young.'

'That's not true. Think of Aunt Primrose. She's never been married at all.'

'She's a spinster.'

'My, my, that's a word *I* never taught you. And there was I, thinking they teach you nothing at school except how to sing "Rule Britannia".'

'I learned "spinster" from Freddy Harris.'

'He's a stupid boy. You've got more brain-power in a hair that falls off your head than he has inside his whole skull.'

Which gave me a new conundrum to worry about: did one lose tiny amounts of brain-power every time one's hairs fell out? Was that why very old, bald people tended to be daft?

'Why did you stop exploring?' I asked my mother.

'I haven't stopped,' she said. 'I'm exploring more than ever. This is the strangest country of all.'

I couldn't disagree with her there.

★   ★   ★

Intimate as we were, I didn't tell Mama that another boy had taught me a different word for what Aunt Primrose was: *unnatural*. Aunt Primrose lived with us in our house. She had always lived with us, even in Australia, even before I was born. She was a good five years older than my mother but, looking at photographs of her now, I can appreciate what I had no conception of then: that she was an extraordinarily beautiful woman. More beautiful, certainly, than my mother, who, although she had big blue eyes, also had a slight double chin, a slightly protruding brow, and unruly, fleecy blonde hair. Aunt Primrose was blessed with perfect features, an exquisitely sculptured neck, chocolate brown eyes, a glossy swirl of dark hair that stayed obediently in place. A few decades earlier, she might have been a muse for the Pre-Raphaelites, although they would have insisted she wear a figure-hugging velvet dress with an embroidered bodice. The Edwardian years were not conducive to such things.

It was a bad time for women's fashions, to be frank. My mother customarily wore what just about every female of her class wore: a plain white blouse, cut wide and shapeless, to accommodate the unsupported bosom which hung low, muffled by undergarments, so that her torso resembled a pigeon's. Her blouse she tucked into an ankle-length grey skirt reined in tight at the belt. In my toddler years, I remember her looking fantastically impressive in fox furs, but shortly after arriving in England, she came home from a mysterious public meeting (she was always attending mysterious meetings) and declared that killing foxes was wicked. That was the end of the big cuddly pelts I'd adored. Instead, she took to wearing a long black woollen coat that had all the style of a cabhorse's feedbag. Inside the house, she wore her hair in a continually unravelling bun; out of doors, she wore a hat that could have served as a cushion on a piano stool.

Aunt Primrose, by contrast, was always immaculately tailored. So why did my schoolmates regard her as *unnatural*? Because her tailoring was masculine, that's why. She favoured formal suit jackets and frock coats, altered slightly to give a subtle feminine puff to the shoulders or a swell to the bosom, but essentially no different from the garb of august parliamentarians. She even wore a fob watch. I never perceived it as mannish at the time. I was too accustomed to seeing Aunt Primrose together with Mama on the divan, laughing and lolling about. In my eyes she was soft and kittenish, a million miles removed from the men who walked stiffly through my daily life, the dour schoolmasters and glum crossing-sweepers and grim policemen. But, looking at a photograph of her at the remove of fifty years, I am startled by the unwomanly directness of her gaze. *Who are you to judge me?* she seems to be saying to the photographer, as she poses in a dressing-gown, high-collared shirt and cravat.

I always called her Auntie, never Primrose. My mother called her Poss. She called my mother Sophie.

Where did my father fit in this arrangement? Apart, that is, from having made half of me? I am still not sure. He called my mother Dear Heart, always Dear Heart. But he said it somewhat distractedly, the way men talk to themselves when they are busy with an absorbing task. Or he would pronounce it with waggish emphasis, mocking what she was asking of him, and she would respond with an irritable upwards puff from her pouting lip, blowing the loose curls off her brow.

My father, although hairy and deep-voiced, was not very tall, and, like Aunt Primrose, failed to meet the standards of normality set by my English schoolmates. He was an artist, for one thing: a painter. Other people's houses were full of knick-knacks, china and the smell of potpourri; ours was full of books, half-finished canvases, old rags stiff with dried paint, and the whiff of turpentine. Not that we were any less well-off than the people with the knick-knacks and the china, mind you. We were securely middle-class. But nobody discussed money in those days, so I have very little idea how our comfortable existence was supported, other than that my father would occasionally get a commission to paint someone's portrait, which would put him into a foul mood and provoke him to impassioned speeches on the sanctity of pure artistic expression. 'Filthy lucre!' he would mutter, kicking at any loose object that had the misfortune to be lying on the floor. I guessed that 'lucre' must be some sort of dirt traipsed into the house off the mucky London streets.

I think Mama had an inheritance. A sizable amount of money had apparently been left to us by an enigmatic figure called Miss Sugar, who came up in murmured conversation only when I was judged safely out of earshot. Miss Sugar: what a name! Speaking it now, I have to admit it sounds like a figment of fantasy, halfway towards Father Christmas or the Tooth Fairy. Can it have been genuine, I wonder? All I can say is that in the late-night reminiscences I overheard in my childhood, Miss Sugar was discussed as a real person, my mother's steadfast travelling companion during their exploration of the world.

Ah, but I've allowed all these larger-than-life females to distract me from my father, as always. My father . . . what was my father, apart from a painter? He was . . . he was a *bohemian*. Again, this was not a word my mother taught me. I learned it from Mr Dalhousie, a master at my school, who pronounced it as if his tongue had been smeared with aniseed. My father was disqualified from the company of men like Mr Dalhousie, because he slept late in the mornings, and spent much of his day squeezing paint onto palettes, scratching his beard, pacing the floor of his studio absentmindedly tossing a peach from one hand to the other, and taking naps.

When I recall him to mind, I rarely see him in a suit, although he was capable of putting on a suit when he left the house. But he rarely left the house. There was almost nothing he wanted to do out there, beyond visiting a few art galleries or popping into the tobacconist's. Even his art materials he selected by post from suppliers he trusted, without the bother of traipsing across town. He preferred to wander from room to room in our little house in Calthorpe Street, his eyes perpetually focused at a height which, had there been a person standing before him, would have been crotch-level. He liked to wear crude workman's trousers and a loose shirt with paint-spattered sleeves. His paintings depicted men dressed similarly informally, reclining against trees in a forest, or on the banks of a river, accompanied by naked women. He never tired of this theme. There must have been dozens of canvases stacked against each other in a corner of the studio, perhaps a hundred or more naked women and clothed men rubbing against each other, some long-dry, others still slightly wet. None of these paintings was ever sold.

My father's portraits were a different matter. In these, he combined (as a contemporary critic admiringly put it) 'innovation with exercise of skill, as though a modern master like John Singer Sargent had been touched by Fauvism and was none the worse for it'. I am still not sure what this means, but I do remember my father's portraits very well.

He was careful with the faces, had a flair for skin, and liked to take liberties with the sitters' clothing. Dresses would blur into impressionistic designs, shoes would be dark smudges. Sometimes, if he was obliged to paint a whole family of daughters, the hands of those he considered less interesting would have ambiguous numbers of fingers. Legs and arms were often longer than anatomically feasible. Most customers were satisfied, though, feeling that they had immortalised themselves in a nobler medium than photography, and that they had patronised a rising star of the avant-garde to boot. But as it turned out, my father's star rose straight through the smoky sky above Bloomsbury, into oblivion.

We weren't to know that, then. My father was the head of our household. He had a job. My mother and Aunt Primrose didn't have jobs, unless working for suffragette organisations was a job. I suppose it was. You know, I grew up awfully confused about work and what it was and who was supposed to do it and who wasn't. Some of the children at Torrington Infants were of the opinion that gentlemen and ladies didn't work: not working was what *made* them gentlemen and ladies. The more prevalent view, by 1908, as far as I could determine, was that men ought to be gainfully employed, but that ladies should not be paid for anything they did, or at least shouldn't *need* paying. The legions of women who laboured in factories and shops were seen as unfortunates; their only claim to dignity was that they hadn't descended into beggary or prostitution. As for domestic servants, I just couldn't figure out what they were about at all. Our family employed a maid-of-all-work, even though Mama and Aunt Primrose thought servants were an offence to socialism. Rachel, her name was, I think. She rarely spoke.

But, getting back to my father . . . Mama and Aunt Primrose always treated him with affectionate condescension, as if he were a dog. An occasionally infuriating, improperly house-trained, but always amusing dog. He played up to them, as a dog might. He had a way of adjusting his big brown eyes that made them glisten imploringly when he was hungry. He slept wherever he chose. Indeed, he slept in so many locations throughout the house that I never developed any conception of 'the bed' as a shrine of marital intimacy. That's why I'm wary of telling people that Mama and Aunt Primrose shared a bed, and that my mother and father slept together only occasionally. Sex: that's all people think about nowa-days, and the more deviant, the better. It wasn't like that in our household. At a certain time of night, when Mama and Auntie Poss had grown tired of talking about female suffrage and the evils of the government, they would shuffle off to bed, and per-haps find my father snoring there like a Great Dane. In which case, they would simply make the best of things. There is no need to see hanky-panky every-where. It's true that my mother and Aunt Primrose often kissed and hugged, but not as often as Mama cuddled me, and you would be surprised how many women in that era were all over each other. It was quite normal. And as for the state of my parents' marriage, well, I exist, don't I? It took two to make me.

Oh, and I may have misrepresented my father by comparing him to a dog. I don't mean to imply that he was without authority. He was a male, after all, and in that era it was a man's world. There were almost daily circumstances in which females were reminded that they did not, and would never, hold the reins of power. Official letters concerning our family, our house, our expenditures, my schooling, new opening hours for Camden Public Library, and

every other imaginable thing, were invariably
addressed to my father. Bureaucrats, tradesmen,
doctors, postmen, parsons, waiters, porters, the
whole pack of them: they ignored my mother and
Aunt Primrose, and directed their remarks to my
father.

Oddly, my mother and Aunt Primrose didn't
seem to mind. 'Time to unsheathe your mighty
sabre, Gilbert,' they would say, if there was an irri-
tating man at the door who obstinately refused to
speak to them. Or they would set Papa against the
vile minions of bureaucracy. I have a vivid memory
of my mother sitting on the parlour floor, using
Aunt Primrose's legs as a support for her back, while
the two of them perused the day's post. 'Here's one
from that horrid little gargoyle at the public
library,' my mother said, resting her head in the lap
of Aunt Primrose's skirt, the better to display the
important-looking letter she held above her face.
She recited the words with mocking pomposity, in
the same voice she used for Humpty Dumpty when
reading me *Through The Looking Glass*. '"It pains me
to have to point out what I assure you I should never
make so bold as to allege, had I not confirmed the
truth of it beyond doubt, for each book borrowed

from this library is checked rigorously upon its return, and any damage immediately noted. Thus, with great regret and no small embarrassment, I am obliged to alert you to the fact that your wife has defaced the book she borrowed from us on the 21st, viz, *Female Education and the Health of the Nation*, by Dr Lucius Hogg, inscribing all manner of disparaging and, frankly, indecent glosses in the margins."' Here the two women dissolved in fits of giggles. 'Well, there's another job for Gilbert,' said my mother, tossing the letter into the air. The following week, a written apology arrived from the library, and the women squirmed and squealed in delight.

People ask me nowadays how I felt, being the son of a bluestocking. I never gave it a thought. My mother's vigorous advocacy of the rights of women seemed natural, a part of her personality, like a dislike of tapioca pudding or a fondness for snow. And, because I was always known as a *child* or a *boy* or a *poppet* or Snookums or Angel or simply Henry, I did not perceive myself to be under attack when Mama or Aunt Primrose railed against those appalling creatures, *men*.

I must make clear, too, that Mama was not a

spiteful person, and her quarrel with the masculine
world was based on indignation rather than hatred.
She liked to collide violently with males who annoyed
her, push them over if she could, and move on. She
and Aunt Primrose worked as a kind of music hall
duo, Mama getting by on charm and disarming hon-
esty, while Aunt Primrose supplied the sardonic
touch. My father was – if you'll excuse what's definitely not meant as a pun – the straight man. When
we lived abroad, I never had the sense of our family
being troublemakers. In Australia, everybody seemed
to be arguing all the time, and enjoying it. Only when
we re-settled in England did I get the impression that
disagreement could be a scandal. And this took a
while for me to learn. At first, I relished the fact that
all sorts of funny new people were wont to make an
appearance at our home, blustering in surprise and
mortification at the things my parents said and did.
But, in the months leading up to June 21st, 1908, the
mood of these visits became increasingly sour, and I
began, little by little, to sense that my family was
caught up in a long and bitter war, and that there
might be casualties.

I remember one such occasion unusually clearly.
Aunt Primrose had invited a wealthy woman called

Felicity to dinner, and Felicity had brought her husband Mr Brown along. Aunt Primrose was involved with a number of charitable organisations and was always on the lookout for patrons; she probably had her eye on Felicity as a potential opening into the fortune Mr Brown had made with his shoe factories.

The after-dinner phase of the evening got off to a convivial start. Mr Brown and my father smoked cigars and discussed Art, a subject on which Mr Brown, a self-made Mancunian, was earnestly attempting to broaden his horizons. The two men drifted in and out of the parlour, exchanging the occasional pleasantry with the three women, who were talking of the future of the world, the reformation of society, and ladies' shoes. I had half-hidden myself behind the dining-room table, and pretended to read storybooks, revelling in the late hour. Eventually, with the aid of good red wine, my mother began to reminisce about the childhood experiences that had made her what she was today.

'When I was a little girl,' she said, 'my father took me on an outing with him, to Lambeth. We had our own carriage, and I was very excited to be seeing the big wide world.'

'The fabled towers of Lambeth,' murmured Aunt
Primrose, with a smirk.

'I'd never been across the Thames,' my mother
continued. 'It seemed as exotic as America. My father
had some business to attend to there. I saw his . . .'
And then she smiled and shook her head, as she
always did when she brushed up against something
in her past that must remain a secret.

'His what, I'm sorry?' said Felicity Brown.

'There was a lot of traffic,' said my mother,
ignoring the question, 'and our coachman took
detours through the poorer streets. The houses
were all jumbled together and falling apart, with
people's underclothes and bedsheets hung in plain
view. I could scarcely believe it. I'd seen poor people
before – hawkers and knife-sharpeners and so on –
and I knew they wore shabby clothes and smelt
sour. But I thought they went home to picturesque
little cottages.'

'Like gingerbread houses,' suggested Felicity
Brown.

'Exactly. The truth filled me with awe. I had my
face poking out of the window of the coach, staring
like a puppy. We passed through a horrible street,
the worst. There was a little girl playing with a

MICHEL FABER

bucket. She was barefoot, almost naked, dressed in a ragged, filthy shirt.'

My mother tipped back her head and squinted, as though peering through a telescope into a long-ago that still existed.

'I thought she looked exactly like me: a mirror image. Perhaps I was wrong; I hadn't seen many children my own age. But I was gripped by a powerful sense that this grubby urchin was someone I might have been, had I been born in that street. Then she picked up a piece of . . . of dog foul, and flung it at me. Her aim was very good, I must say. She hit me right between the eyes.'

Aunt Primrose snorted with laughter, and Felicity Brown, confused, allowed herself a muted chuckle.

'I think I was destined to be a socialist from that moment on,' concluded my mother.

'Nonsense,' said Aunt Primrose. 'Someone else might have experienced exactly the same thing, and decided forever afterwards to grind the poor under her heel. As revenge.'

'Revenge is ugly,' my mother declared. 'It makes me think of military men with small eyes and epaulettes.'

Aunt Primrose, who was not averse to a bit of revenge when it was carried off with aplomb, didn't let Mama get away with this pious stance. 'You once told me you eat spicy food as revenge for the blandness of what you were fed as a child.'

My mother stuck her tongue out at Aunt Primrose, an action that had never seemed particularly rude in Australia, but to which Felicity Brown reacted with a small, startled jerk of her head, as though someone had just vomited.

'All right then,' said my mother, 'let's all get revenge for boiled mutton, mashed potatoes and milk pudding. They deserve it. They caused me much more misery than a turd in the face.'

I knew that the word *turd* was forbidden in polite company, and that the fact that my mother had just tossed it into the conversation meant that things were perhaps getting out of hand. This impression was confirmed when Mr Brown joined us, just at the point when Mama was railing against heartless politicians and exploitative factory owners. Mrs Brown struggled manfully – womanfully? – to smooth the waters my mother was stirring up. Then Mr Brown – who, by this time, had drunk quite a lot of wine – became irritable, defending the right of factory owners to operate competitively in a competitive market. To which my mother retorted that competition was a typically male obsession, which we would all be better off without, in the better world to come. Mr Brown challenged her to explain how this better world would be created, and my mother, egged on by Primrose (who had evidently given up on her daydreams of seducing the Browns into sponsorship) held forth on politics. The Labour Party, she said, had fielded only two successful candidates in its debut election, but only six years later, they got twenty-nine MPs in, which they were sure to increase to a hundred next time round. This made Mr Brown lose his temper.

'Wake up, woman!' he exclaimed. 'The Labour Party will never get anywhere! It's a simple principle of Evolution! A half-educated ape climbs one rung of the ladder and joins the Labour Party; then he climbs a few rungs higher and sees the broader picture . . .'

'You mean, sees how many poor folk are being whipped and starved to produce his bananas?'

'Bananas grow on trees, I believe. And your "poor folk" are rendered less poor when we pay them good money to pick the bananas off.'

'Sounds like paradise, Mr Brown, with a three-penny bonus,' hissed my mother, her face flushed with excitement. 'Oh, the bounty of Mother Nature! Everything falling off the trees! Your watch-chain from the watch-chain tree, your waistcoat from the waistcoat tree, your carriage from the carriage-patch. Tell me when the next shoe crop is ripe, Mr Brown, and we'll go shoe-gathering together!'

The silence that followed this exchange was very unpleasant, but Aunt Primrose had a special knack for breaking such silences with just the right remark.

'I don't care for bananas,' she said, with a naughty twinkle in her eye. 'Peeling them is always more pleasurable than consuming them.'

Mr Brown folded his arms across his chest. His wife glanced somewhat forlornly towards the hallway, where her overcoat hung on a wrought-iron stand.

'You ladies can be as cynical as you like,' said Mr Brown. 'I can't compete with your witty talk. But I understand human nature, and the plain fact is that as soon as a man attains the basic comforts, he no longer fancies marching in a mob of sweaty ruffians, waving banners in the street.'

'Oh, come now: which of us is being cynical?'

'Realistic.'

'Realistic for whom?'

'The human race.'

'Oh? And who decides who's in that?'

My mother was so wound up she might have prolonged the dispute deep into the night, but suddenly my father spoke.

'Well, Mr Brown,' he said calmly, 'I'm a man, and I've attained the basic comforts, but next Sunday I shall be marching in the street, holding up my end of a banner.'

I don't recall what was said after that, if anything. I don't recall by what magical means the Browns were whisked out of our house, never to return. I only recall the fierce affection with which Mama embraced Papa. Her clutching hands went white against his back. Their cheeks were squashed together. I thought he would surely collapse from lack of breath. But they stood together like that for what seemed like half an hour. Then Aunt Primrose yawned, said 'Well done, Gilbert,' and curled up to sleep on the sofa.

I know your curiosity is aroused now. I know you want to know about the march. Perhaps you've read about it in history books. And here I am – 'living history', as they say – and I suppose you're mindful that

I'm ninety-two years old, and I may not have much longer to tell my story. But forgive me: I want to spend a little longer on my parents, and Aunt Primrose, and the way things were for us during that strange season when we settled in England.

Nowadays, I suppose they'd call it culture shock. I missed everything about where I had come from. I missed breathing the air. I missed the tree-lined, leaf-strewn roads of Mount Macedon, which we would travel along when returning to Melbourne from Aunt Primrose's brother's house. I missed the balmy afternoons picnicking in the Botanic Gardens. I missed the smell of eucalyptus. Apples and pears tasted all wrong, and the London drinking-water had scum on it, which Mama assured me was not dirt, but lime. The magnificent clear Victorian skies – that is, Victoria the place, not Victoria the English queen – had been foolishly swapped for the damp, smutty atmosphere of a polluted metropolis. There was nowhere to play in Bloomsbury and (here was another bombshell) I must cease talking to strangers. Imagine that! In Australia, if I played too long in the uncultivated outskirts of our neighbourhood, and the sun set on me, a stranger was liable to escort me home. In London, a stranger was liable (if I believed my mother's warnings) to pull me into a dark alley, strip me naked, and sell my clothes in Petticoat Lane. Another anxiety to be added to the list of this country's demerits!

I complained about these things to my mother one afternoon, intimating that we may have made a mistake, and that it might be a good idea to climb aboard a boat at our soonest convenience and sail for home.

My mother motioned for me to climb into her lap instead. She cradled me against her bosom, which was big and soft, even though she was not a big woman. She stroked me so tenderly I could sense she was about to cause me pain.

'Life can't always be as we wish,' she said.

'Why not?' I said.

'Things happen.'

'Us coming here didn't happen. We didded it. *You* didded it.'

'Did, darling. We *did* it.'

She stroked my hair, smoothing it over my ears. I shrugged irritably, pretending to be ticklish.

'Is our house in Australia still there?'

'Of course it's still there, angel. Houses don't just fall down.'

'Well, why can't we go back there?'

'Because . . . because we left.' She could tell from the way I squirmed that I found this answer highly unsatisfactory. It was a Mad Hatter answer, a March Hare answer. Mama couldn't expect to read me the *Alice* books a hundred times and get away with such nonsense.

'A house only manages to be a home for a while,' she said at last. 'Being a home isn't easy. Houses get tired.'

I punched her breast, as hard as I could, in frustration. The violence of it shocked us both. She hugged me tighter to her.

'Listen,' she said. 'Listen. I'm going to tell you something I haven't told anyone except Poss and your father. You must promise never to tell a soul.'

I didn't promise. I suppose she took my silence as a promise. And now I'm breaking that silence, by telling you, because I can't see that it matters anymore. Everyone in this story passed away long ago, and soon I'll be history too. But then, we're all history, aren't we? History is all of us, end to end, until . . . well, the end. Which is exactly the sort of half-sensical platitude I suspected my mother of trying to pacify me with when I punched her.

'The truth is,' she said, 'that it isn't true what I told you, that I was born in a tiny village in the countryside. I was born in London. In a house only a few miles from here. I lived there until I was seven. Then I was . . . I was removed. My governess took me away. I thought we would come back. But we didn't come back.'

'Why didn't your Mama and Papa stop her?'

'My Mama wasn't alive by then. And my Papa . . . I don't know. I don't know. Home wasn't home anymore. Please try to understand. Home isn't a house. Home is a feeling of being safe somewhere, and I didn't feel safe with my father. So my governess and I went out into the world, looking . . .' She left a long pause, not breathing, as though the rest of the sentence was already on her tongue, poised to roll off. Then she laid her cheek against the top of my head and sighed. 'Looking.'

'She was against the law, wasn't she, your governess?' I said.

Mama chuckled softly. 'I'm sure she was.'

'The police should have arrested her.'

'That thought did occur to me, eventually. When I was about fourteen. Poor Miss Sugar . . . I gave her such lectures about morality! There she'd be, serving me my breakfast, and there I'd be, with my nose in my uncle's battered old Bible, sulking.'

Somehow, with my body, I must have let my mother know that I was comprehending none of this. At once, she put aside her grown-up musings, and found a morsel I could digest, a bon-bon for a little boy.

'Police have better things to do, angel,' she said, 'than to arrest defenceless women. They have robbers and murderers to catch.'

That satisfied me for a while. It was only days later, when my mother and Aunt Primrose were discussing the imminent release of one of their suffragette friends from Holloway Prison, that I remembered that policemen could, and did, arrest defenceless females. Evidently there were not enough robbers and murderers to keep them busy.

Only with hindsight does it seem surprising that my mother never got arrested herself. She, like the semi-mythical Miss Sugar, was against the law in various ways. For instance, she would scandalise me terribly sometimes, when we went out together, by stealing books from bookshops. Her technique, while not exactly brazen, lacked the stealthy finesse of a talented shoplifter. She would simply stuff the book inside her coat – using me as cover, it now occurs to me – and saunter out of the shop. Then she would walk straight to the nearest drain-hole and slip the book through, helping it on its way with her toe if it got stuck. The books were always about women and 'the female question'. Mama relished the sound they made when they hit the sewer-water below.

My mother also regularly volunteered to go out on the streets to sell *Votes For Women*, a penny newspaper, and she walked defiantly on the footpath with it, which meant she could be charged with 'obstruction'. Looking back on it, you'd think that a woman selling a newspaper in traffic would cause a damn sight more obstruction than if she did it on the footpath, but there you are: that was how the Powers That Be decided it. It was all cat-and-mouse stuff, of course. But my mother refused to be a mouse. 'I will not walk in the gutter,' she said, when counselled by her more law-fearing friends to do so. 'I will not.' And she never did – except, of course, when disposing of books with titles like *The Natural Destiny of the Female*.

I hope I'm not giving the impression that my

mother got her way in everything, nor that people in Authority always turned a blind eye to her transgressions. She had her share of mishaps. But whenever she was thwarted, she would look at her tormentor – policeman, petty official, shopkeeper, whatever – as if he were a pitiable madman, whose mission was to prevent people doing something unobjectionably innocent like drinking tea or trimming their toenails. Aunt Primrose, by contrast, was more easily grieved, despite her cool exterior. The droll self-assurance she displayed in public was apt to break down in private, and I would often run into the house, flushed with childish enthusiasm for something-or-other, only to find Aunt Primrose curled up in an armchair, furiously sucking on a cigarette, tears trickling down her cheeks. Or, if the Government had just behaved with exceptional malice or cowardice, I would hear her yelling 'How could they! How could they!' and so on. 'Don't let them get to you, Poss,' my Mama would say, laying her arm over her friend's shoulder. 'Never let them get to you.'

Only twice did I see Mama reduced to tears by frustration. The first time was over what seemed to me a trifle. Newly returned to England, exploring

Regent Street with me, she went into a department store and asked if they stocked a particular brand of perfume. The shopwalker told her that they did not. My mother insisted: it's a very renowned manufacturer, she said. I have never heard of it, madam, said the shopwalker. That's impossible, said my mother: what about the soaps and bathwater? The shopwalker apologised and said he had never heard of this particular brand; perhaps it was something exclusively available in Australia? (He could tell from her accent that she had spent some years in the colonies.) At this point my mother's lip started to tremble, and when the shopwalker, in an attempt to pacify her, offered to sell her a bottle of Pears' lavender water, she uttered a strange choking sound, and fled out of the store. I had never seen her behave so childishly in Australia; it was one of the first incidents I took as proof that we should never have crossed the ocean.

But that decision, as I was only too painfully aware, was not mine to make or unmake. In telling me about her abduction by Miss Sugar, my mother had reminded me that children are subject to the will of grown-ups, and cannot choose where they live or where they go. How clever she was to have that little heart-to-heart with me! Was it deliberate, I wonder? She made me believe that my outburst of grief had pushed her to reveal her most secret memories, memories too intimate to be shared with anyone but me, Papa and Aunt Primrose. How special I felt! – even as she was telling me that my wishes counted for nothing. How vulnerable she seemed, as she recalled her childish bewilderment at the way her life had been turned upside down. It was enough to make me forget that she'd shown no mercy in overturning my own.

However. There's no point blaming her now, is there? We emigrated, and that was how it was. The colonies went their own sweet way, and we went ours, and I have become, for good or ill, an Englishman. Last of the old-fashioned gentlemen, as the nurses here call me! And of course I learned, in the fullness of time, that my mother was right. Life defies our intentions to be rational; it misleads and teases us until we are driven to do foolish things. I know. Oh God, I know.

But you don't want to hear about my life. You want to hear about the march. I'm getting to that, I really am. I give you my solemn promise I won't die before finishing the story. I do understand how maddening it is to get only so far, and not know what happened next. I wouldn't do that to you!

The first thing to be said is that, as a boy of seven, I had only the haziest notions of what all this was about. My parents had been discussing the march and its importance for months, but mostly amongst themselves, and so they felt free to use words like 'franchise', 'empowerment', 'Asquith', 'progressive' and 'suffrage', whereas I preferred words like 'play', 'eat', 'toffee-apple' and 'kiss'. 'Suffrage' was something I thought people experienced when they got sick or when a horse kicked them.

As for marching, I had been under the impression that it was something only soldiers did. Yet Mama and Aunt Primrose were counting down the days to the 21st of June, when they would do their duty. I wondered how they would manage the strides, in their long skirts, and whether Mama might trip on the cobbles. (She was shorter than Aunt Primrose, and her boots had quite a heel on them.)

My father was an integral part of the preparations for this momentous event. He had helped the ladies paint a banner – the only collaborative artistic endeavour he'd ever undertaken, I believe – which resulted in Mama getting green paint all over her hair. The banner turned out very handsome, though. VOTES FOR WOMEN, it said, in green, white and purple, the colours of the Women's Social and Political Union. Green for hope, white for purity and purple for dignity. On either side of the inscription, my father had painted a statuesque woman in a long, flowing dress, with a helmet on her head and a trumpet in her hand. It strikes me now that these two Amazons may well have been the only female figures, apart from the ladies in his portrait commissions, to gain entry into my father's oeuvre with their clothes on.

There were in fact two marches that June, within a week of each other. The first was organised by the National Union of Women's Suffrage Societies, and, as far as I'm aware, my family didn't go. I've since learned, from history books, that the NUWSS favoured polite, constitutional, law-abiding means of change. That doesn't sound like my parents' style, I must admit. The June 21st march was organised by the Women's Social and Political Union, a far more militant group. They were the ones who published the penny newspaper my mother sold in the street. They were the ones who had the champion colours (the other team had red and white, which my father dismissed as a crude combination). They were the ones who interrupted gentlemen's political meetings, got arrested, got thrown into prison. Sensational! In our household, Emmeline, Christabel, Sylvia and Adela Pankhurst were heroines on a par with Hercules. Not that Hercules was a woman, but you know what I mean.

The march would have been exciting enough for me had I merely heard tell of it and seen the lovely banner my Mama and Papa had made together. But I was actually going to be a participant. I was going to be there, in Hyde Park! I would march with my father and my mother and Auntie Primrose, and the prime minister would peep from behind the curtains of his palace and tremble in fear, and then the laws would change. It was all fantastically thrilling; my only worry was how I would cope with the physical demands of the march, since my legs were a great deal shorter than grown-ups'.

How fortunate, then, that my new school took my training in hand. Clearly, Torrington Infants was well aware of the impending challenge and was determined to ensure that its pupils were up to it. A few weeks before the big day, a rigorous, vigorous

system of exercises was introduced to our curri-
culum, to make us hale of lung and strong of limb.
At the peal of a bell, we boys, uniformly dressed in
our grey caps, grey worsted jackets buttoned up to
the neck, grey knickerbockers, long black socks and
black shoes, would be marched out of the class-
rooms. We would tramp round the school building
twice, kept in rhythm by our master chanting 'Left,
right, left, right.' Then we would assemble in the
quadrangle, shivering in the chill of an English
summer morning, and our master would instruct us
to do battle with the air. We'd fling our arms and
legs about, lift our knees up to our chests, pirou-
ette, salute the sickly sun with our ink-stained little
hands. Half-hearted gestures were not allowed;
anyone failing to strike a strenuous pose was
instantly barked at.

I was able to perform well enough, but I felt sorry
for some of my schoolmates who couldn't – in
particular, a wretched lad called Jerome who had a
club foot that he was forced to heave off the ground,
and another boy whose name I forget, who would
spurt snot and blood from his nose whenever he bent
to touch his toes. You know, I've been an eye-witness
to some truly historic things in my life – the Great

Floods of 1928, for example, or the first Olympic Games after Hitler, at Wembley in 1948 – and can barely remember them, but until my dying day I will have a picture-perfect recollection of that poor boy's socks as he seated himself at his desk each morning: flaccid, furry, misshapen, pinkish grey, from his mother's nightly attempts to wash the blood out of the wool.

And yet, however much pity I felt for these poor lads, I was grateful that my physical fitness was being improved for its June 21st appointment. Grateful for a couple of weeks, at least. Like the notion that my mother and father had taken turns to fashion my top and bottom half, my conviction that Torrington Infants School wanted to help me march with the suffragettes was shortlived. And this time, it wasn't my mother who enlightened me to my mistake, but my father. I mentioned my participation in the exercises at my school, and assured him that I was confident that, come the day of reckoning, I would be able to keep pace. He laughed. He told me that my school's exercise programme was all because the British Army had put on a poor show in a war against the bores (or that's how I understood it) and there was now widespread fear that the nation's young were puny and enfeebled. In schools all across the country, he said, children like me were being arranged into little battalions, to learn how to march to war and engage in hand-to-hand combat with future enemies.

'Who shall I have to fight, Papa?' I asked.

He smiled, cupped his hand over my head, and wiggled my skull affectionately.

'Your Mama and I will make sure you shan't ever have to fight anyone, Henry. We are specialists in escape.'

'But who will be the enemies?' I persisted. 'Is there a war coming soon?' I knew about wars; I had seen paintings of them in art galleries with my Papa, giant pictures of sword-brandishing Italians and chariots and circus animals and wounded horses and flaming fortresses, lacquered with what looked like nine coats of furniture polish.

My father laughed. 'It's already here!' he said. 'The war between rich and poor, the war between employers and workers . . . Oh, and let's not forget the war between men and women!'

Pleased as I was to see my father laughing, I was unnerved by this last comment.

'You won't ever fight Mama, will you, Papa?'

He laughed again.

'Your Mama and I are on the same side, Henry. Always on the same side. Remember that.'

I did.

Now, as I promised, the day of the march . . . The day of the march . . . You know, it's a bit like the 1948 Olympics. One feels a tremendous responsibility to recall everything in detail, because one was there, and it was a key moment in History. But for me, the march was only one of many key moments in the history of our family – in the history of my mother and me. Oh, don't fret: I remember a respectable amount. I'm not going to suddenly claim that the entire day is a blank. But some of it has gone missing.

What I wore, for example. Odd, that. I still have an after-image, in my mind's eye, of the socks I mentioned earlier, the socks of that poor lad whose nose bled all the time, but if I try to picture what my Mama dressed me in for this wonderfully special occasion, I draw a blank. My school clothes? My Sunday best? I don't recall if I even *had* a Sunday outfit. My family, despite Mama's sentimental attachment to her uncle Henry's Bible, were not churchgoers. In fact, Sunday the 21st of June, 1908, was probably the first time we'd ever attended any solemn ceremony as a family, and we were going to the Church of Female Suffrage.

Mama wore her long black feedbag coat, as always, and her shapeless piano-cushion hat. Aunt Primrose was decked out in the colours of the WSPU: snow-white skirt and blouse, purple jacket with white buttons and green cuffs, green chapeau decorated with a sprig of lavender. She'd even bought a purple umbrella, but left it at home because the weather that morning was cloudless and brilliant. My father wore his usual outdoors suit, augmented with a neckerchief that might or might not have been green. I'm glad he didn't wear white, green and purple; it would have been unmanly. He carried the banner and the two long poles it was sewn onto, rolled up under his arm. It must have been jolly heavy, but his face betrayed no effort.

We walked to the junction of Gray's Inn Road and, to my surprise and delight, were fetched from there by a float of suffragettes. The float was drawn by two horses in gay head-dress, with a female at the reins (sensational!), and had about a dozen women on board already. VOTES FOR WOMEN flags and pennants hung off it on all sides, fluttering in the breeze. The women were smiling and excited, chattering amongst themselves. One of them reached down to me from her perch and helped me clamber up. We were off.

Perhaps I shouldn't have been so amazed at our smoothly synchronised transport. The demonstration was, as I learned much later, a triumph of planning, a fearsomely premeditated campaign on a military scale. A thousand pounds had been spent on publicity, a vast sum in those days. There can scarcely have been a woman in Britain who hadn't been informed when, where and how to participate. Thirty special trains had ferried demonstrators from all over the country. There were seven separate processions snaking towards Hyde Park through London's major thoroughfares. Our little float of suffragettes was part of an army 30,000 strong.

Of course, many more people came to watch. More than a quarter of a million, in fact. As we trotted further into the city, my eyes goggled at the sheer profusion of human beings. They were thronging on the pavements, jostling on balconies, poking out of windows, standing on rooftops, clinging to lampposts, popping up from signs that said THROUGH THICK & THIN WE NE'R GIVE

IN and COLMAN'S MUSTARD. Instinctively, even though I was on top of the float and in no danger of being crushed, I shrank back. My mother – I assume it was my mother, maybe it was one of the other women – put her arm around my chest and hugged me from behind. The woman next to me introduced herself, shouting to be heard above the hubbub of the crowd and the blaring of the brass band that paraded in front of us. She said her name was Emily. I wonder now: can this have been Emily Wilding Davison, who, five years later, would become the first suffragette martyr, trampled under the hooves of the King's horse? If so, she looked remarkably cheerful to me that Sunday morning.

'This,' she said, waving her white-gloved hand at the multitudes, 'is something they can't tear up and throw in the waste-paper basket.' I didn't know what she meant, but her confidence was infectious. I smiled and nodded, and she patted my knee lingeringly.

I don't recall the moment when we parted company from Emily and the other ladies on the float. The next thing I remember is marching with my parents in the midst of a vast sea of people. I needn't have worried about keeping up: we moved very slowly, much more slowly than I was made to march at Torrington Infants. More like a stroll, really, except that the music of the brass bands and the thunderous din of the crowd reminded me that this was a magnificently important occasion. What route did we take to Hyde Park? I haven't the foggiest. I was three feet tall. There were thousands of adult bodies around me. Mama and Papa were walking slowly in step, each holding a pole straight up against their chests, the VOTES FOR WOMEN banner stretched in the air between them. I was bursting with pride. For a while, at least. Then I was bursting to have a pee. No one else seemed to need it, and the multitudes marched on, bearing me along with them.

There is nothing so ruinous to a sense of historical occasion as a full bladder. Jesus Christ could be descending from the heavens arm-in-arm with Helen of Troy, and you'd still be on the lookout for a loo. I remember glancing up at my parents' faces, hoping to catch their eye, but it was no use. Mama, Papa and Aunt Primrose were as erect as they could be, radiant with conviction, focused on the future. It was as though they were prepared to march for days on end, never tiring until they'd achieved everything there was to be achieved. It

was as though they meant to flush the prime minister out of his hiding place and hound him, step
by step, across London until he was obliged to
topple backwards into the Thames. I became increasingly frightened. At one point, the crowd parted
somewhat and I thought we were going to escape
into an open space. But then another procession
marched into view: a mighty horde of women in
very big hats, advancing.

Finally I found the courage to tug at my
mother's coat and tell her I needed to relieve myself.
She had to bend almost double to hear me, the
banner dipping as she leaned her ear against my
lips. She nodded. She handed her pole to Aunt
Primrose, who took hold of it without hesitation.
Primrose and Papa fell into step with each other,
and my mother and I began to squirm our way
through the crowd, swimming at right angles to the
tide.

With each second, I became more convinced that
I was doomed to wet my trousers. Even assuming
that we managed to locate a public toilet, there
would probably be several hundred people queuing
up to use it. But my mother had thought of that.
The nearest bush we came up against (we were in

Hyde Park by this time, evidently), she selected as my urinal.

'I'll shield you,' she said, and turned her back on me, opening her coat wide and flapping it with her hands, as though attempting to cool herself in the broiling heat. I lost no time. Within seconds the leaves of the bush were dripping with my pee. I tapped on the back of Mama's coat, to let her know I was ready to rejoin the fray. She said,

'Now, *you* shield *me*.'

We changed places and she squatted next to the bush. I didn't see what happened next, as I had my back turned. There were people hurrying past constantly: men in cloth caps, men in bowlers, men in boaters, women in WSPU colours, even a pair of policemen who, although they were a good ten yards away, gave me a cold thrill of terror. Nobody looked in our direction, though, and before long I felt my mother's warm hand on my shoulder.

Finding Papa and Aunt Primrose was not going to be easy. The teeming horde had moved on. We hurried to catch up, got snarled in a scrum of men and women engaged in a heated political discussion. The men had been drinking, I think, even though it was Sunday. There was a pretty young lady balanced precariously on a folding chair, very white in the face, clutching her VOTES FOR WOMEN sash tightly in one fist.

'Why don't you (blah blah blah)?' bellowed one of the men. (I couldn't make out what his suggestion was.)

'Because that's not how change has ever happened in this country, sir,' retorted the white-faced lady. 'Women will get the vote in the same way that William the Conquerer got England, or Henry the Eighth got his wives – by crushing the opposition.'

Another man laughed. 'You can crush me anytime, Miss!'

The lady's cheeks turned from white to crimson. She said something, but her voice had lost its power and I couldn't hear the words.

'You won't change Asquith's mind by squeaking in a public park!' yelled another man. 'Now, if you took him to bed . . . !'

The lady bit her lip, looked round at her friends for support. A stocky woman with a stern face waved her hand at the tormentors and exclaimed: 'It's this sort of degenerate behaviour that will be swept away when there are women in Parliament!'

'Humbug!' yelled one of the men.

'Prostitutes!' yelled another. 'You're all whores!'

My mother grabbed me by the hand and we hurried away, in a different direction from the one we'd been pursuing. I presumed she was taking a long way round, reasoning that the crowds were too thick in the middle. But when I chanced to look up at her, I saw that her face had undergone a remarkable transformation. Its glow of excitement faded, leaving her pale and distracted. Her gaze had lost its bright-eyed focus, and flitted over the heads of the crowd, disconsolate. *She's lost without Papa*, I thought.

Suddenly she came to a standstill, her grip on my small hand almost painful.

'There are too many people,' she said – whether to me or to herself, I have no idea. 'I want to go home.' And she turned on her heel, pulling me with her.

'What about Papa?' I cried.

'Don't worry about him,' she said as she strode ahead. 'He's in his element – surrounded by women. He's the hero of the march.'

'What about Auntie Primrose?'

'She has your father with her.'

'Everyone will think she's Mrs Papa.'

'That's not the end of the world.'

Mama was walking awfully fast. I had to run to keep up with her. I'd expected to get footsore from marching, not breathless from sprinting. We barged through the exit, emerged onto a busy street which I suppose must have been Bayswater Road.

Almost instantaneously, my mother hailed a taxi-cab. Only decades later did I appreciate how miraculous that was. Mama seemed to summon it out of nowhere; or rather, it arrived as if in response to her distress, as if the driver – or his horse – had sensed her longing for rescue and hurried to oblige. But when my Mama told the cabbie that she wanted to go to Calthorpe Street, Bloomsbury, he winced as though she'd pricked him in the shoulder with a pin. Bloomsbury lay on the other side of the protesting legions. There were a third of a million bodies to be traversed.

'Ma'am, ain't there somewhere else you'd rather go?' the cabbie said, trying out his charm on this woman who so often relied on charm herself. 'America might be easier. Or North Kensington.'

My mother hesitated. She tilted her head back, and closed her eyes tight, and I could tell she was every bit as tired as I was. Then she said:

'Take me to Notting Hill Gate.'

'A doddle, ma'am. Any particular address?'

'I'm . . . I'm not completely sure,' she said. 'One of the houses in Chepstow Villas.'

'Right you are, ma'am.'

There are so many things a child doesn't ask – even a child who is uncommonly close to his mother. During our lives together I must have asked my Mama a hundred thousand questions: where does the moon go when the sun shines; do spiders dream; what happens to music once it's gone inside your ears; what is water made of; do cameras remember what they've seen; how does the tide decide when to come in; why is money worth money; what are souls for if there is no God. But I never asked why she chose to go to Chepstow Villas on that Sunday afternoon, with me in tow, when she could have gone alone, unobserved, on a day when she wasn't footsore and overwrought. At the time, I assumed she was hoping to visit a friend.

As we trotted out of Kensington and into Notting Hill, my mother became increasingly agitated. She peered out of the window, swinging her head abruptly to the left or right as though fast-moving objects were speeding by, even though the vehicles and pedestrians around us were proceeding at a sedate pace.

'Where's this?' she called to the driver.

'Pembridge Road, madam,' he replied.

'Pembridge Villas?' she called.

'It's called Pembridge Road these days, madam.'

For some reason this seemed to make my mother feel better.

'I suppose everything has changed so much in the last thirty years that it's unrecognisable!' she remarked.

'Oh no, madam,' replied the cabman. 'It's much the same, I'd say. There's more houses near the potteries, but these streets here, they never change.'

This put the frown back on my mother's face. She resumed staring out the window, jerking her head back and forth. Her hands clutched at her knees through the fabric of her dress. To my eye, the houses we were passing were staid, respectable edifices, larger and paler than the ones in Bloomsbury, but typical of the solemn solidity of buildings in the Old Country. To my mother they appeared to be more like playful phantoms, ducking behind one another, running round and round our cab.

'Chepstow Villas, madam,' announced the cabman.

'Already?' said Mama. She blinked stupidly, like Freddy Harris whenever the masters asked him to do a simple sum. I was becoming annoyed with her. The journey had been quite long enough for me. I wanted to collapse into a sofa and be fed warm cocoa and a biscuit.

The two of us were offloaded onto the street. My mother dismissed the cabman with a dignified nod but as soon as she turned her face away from him, the look of anxiety returned. She clearly had no idea where she was.

'I'm tired, Mama,' I said.

She didn't reply, even though I knew she'd heard me. We began walking along the footpath. There was hardly anyone about. It was Sunday afternoon, after all. Ultra-respectable people were indoors reading the Bible, or attending afternoon church services, or secretly gardening. The rest were in the centre of town, probably, rubbernecking to catch a glimpse of the suffragettes on their carnival floats.

Mama was examining the wrought-iron gates of each of the properties in Chepstow Villas. She reached the end of the street without having found what she was looking for, and walked back, more slowly, the other way, this time actually touching some of the gates with the tips of her fingers.

'Yes, yes,' she murmured as she loitered forwards. 'I can see now . . .'

She stopped, turned on her heel, and bowed slightly, like a dancer executing a formal manoeuvre in a ballroom.

'This house,' she said. 'Come with me.'

We approached a façade that was indistinguishable from its neighbours, swung open a small, new-looking gate with spikes on top, and presented ourselves at the front door. My mother rang the bell. After a long while, a middle-aged, well-dressed woman – most definitely not a servant – opened the door, looked my mother up and down.

'I have nothing to discuss with you or your kind,' she said. 'You are unnatural.'

And she shut the door in Mama's face. Mama turned around, looking rather stunned.

'It's all right,' she muttered, principally to herself. 'It wasn't the place anyway. I could see behind her, the shape of the staircase . . . It was all wrong.'

She stood, lost in thought for a few moments. She chewed her bottom lip. She was wondering, I imagine, why the woman had so confidently called her *unnatural*. The answer came to her abruptly. She fumbled to remove her VOTES FOR WOMEN sash, which was ostentatiously draped across her torso. She rolled it up and handed it to me.

'Take care of this for a minute,' she said.

We moved on to the next house. My mother rang the bell. There was no response. She rang the bell again. Again, no response.

'Perhaps the people are at the march,' I suggested.

'Perhaps,' said my mother. She leaned her face close to a stained-glass inlay in the door and tried to peer through, embarrassing me keenly. Anyone might think she was a criminal.

'I don't think this is the place either,' she mumbled. 'It's too small.'

We moved on to the next house. My mother stood and examined it from the footpath for a long time before approaching. She turned her back on it, stepped towards the kerb, eyes half-closed, then turned again, as if freshly arriving. She tilted her head first to the left, until her ear was almost touching her coat-collar, then tilted it just as far to the right. She wiggled her fingers in the air between us and, because she was behaving so oddly, it was some moments before I realised she was motioning for me to take her hand.

'This is the one,' she said. 'I think. I'm almost sure of it. They've replaced the door, that's all. Always replacing things.'

We walked up to the door and Mama rang the bell. A bald man with brilliant blue eyes opened it almost at once. He had a kindly face. It was not the face my mother hoped to see, evidently. She craned her head to look around the man's body, to see farther into the house. I blushed, wishing I were strong enough to grab Mama by the wrist and march her away.

'Excuse me,' she said. 'Is this the house of . . .' (and she lowered her voice to murmur a name).

'I beg your pardon, madam?'

She leaned closer to him and repeated herself. Anyone might have thought she was kissing him.

He smiled and shook his head. 'No one by that name lives here, madam.'

My mother peered longingly over the bald man's shoulder. I swear she made me nervous she would seize hold of his necktie and attempt to climb over his body. Without being able to help it, I craned my neck too, and caught a glimpse of a chandelier, and large paintings of rural scenes hung in the hallway.

'But I know this place,' my mother said.

The bald man shook his head. 'Mr De La Salle lives here now.'

'That's not possible,' said my mother.

'I assure you it's perfectly possible,' said the bald man. 'I am Mr De La Salle.'

'But before you . . . ?'

'Before me, madam, there was a Mrs St John, if memory serves.'

'That's not possible. I can see the door to your sitting room. I *know* that door.'

'With all due respect, madam, it's not our sitting room. It's our dining room.'

'I don't care what you use it for!' blurted my mother.

The bald man opened his mouth to speak, but managed only an exasperated sound half-way between a cough and a sigh. Mama raised her hand, a little too suddenly perhaps, and the man took fright. He stepped nimbly backwards and shut the door. It wasn't a slam exactly, but the click was decisive.

My mother walked wonkily back to the footpath.

She seemed to be having trouble balancing on the high heels of her boots. She sat down near the kerb, right there in full view of the passing vehicles. I could have sunk through the paving-stones and disappeared into the underworld.

'Mama,' I ventured. 'When are we going home?'

My mother didn't get up. Instead, she started to wail like a toddler. She howled and bawled. Her cheeks went red and puffy, tears ran down her face and dripped from her jawline, and a wetness that looked alarmingly like snot glimmered on her lips. She was awfully loud. I stood by, helpless, clutching her VOTES FOR WOMEN sash in my hands. Picking my mama up off the footpath was a task quite beyond my muscle-power; just lifting the clothes would have been difficult enough, without the person inside. I looked around, half-hoping there wouldn't be a soul to witness my mother's fit of anguish, and half-hoping that sympathetic Londoners would be speeding to her aid. I saw one old lady with a sausage dog, quite some way off, hurrying in the opposite direction. I saw a curtain being drawn across one of the windows of Chepstow Villas. My mother howled on.

Rescue came, once more, miraculously. A cab

drove up. Not a horse-drawn cab, a motorised one. A car, in other words. There were already quite a few of them about in those days (indeed, Felicity Brown had arrived at our house in one), but they tended to be owned by people who considered breakdowns all part of the fun and who were in no particular hurry to get anywhere. For serious transportation, horse-drawn cabs were still the norm. But here was a shiny new pea-green motor-cab, emblazoned 'Taxi DeLuxe Company of Kensington', pulling up right next to my mother's convulsing body.

'May I be of assistance, madam?' called the driver.

'Go away,' cried my mother.

'An excellent idea, madam,' rejoined the driver, quick as a flash. 'Where do you fancy going?'

'Nowhere,' cried my mother.

'Mama,' I interjected, 'we need to get home. Papa will be worried. And Auntie Primrose too.'

'Quite right, quite right,' said the cab driver breezily. 'Think of poor old Auntie Primrose. Worried sick, she'll be.'

My mother laughed despite herself. She pulled a handkerchief from her jacket pocket and blew her nose.

'Bloomsbury,' she said.

'*Ooo*-er,' winced the driver. 'Now there's a challenge.'

Mama's face was suddenly composed.

'Why? Isn't your motor up to it?'

The driver patted his steering wheel proudly. 'Fifteen horse-power engine, madam. It could take you to the ends of the earth, with enough fuel.'

'Bloomsbury will do.'

'You know there's been some sort of procession today, I suppose, madam? Thousands of people in the streets. Terrible disruptions.'

'Yes, I know,' said my mother, picking herself up. She dusted off the horrid feedbag coat. Its black fabric showed the dust without mercy. The cab driver leapt off his perch, ushered us into the plushly upholstered cabin. The motor purred, sending a sensuous buzz through the floor, the seats, everything. The mingled smell of leather, newness and engine-oil was like an exotic perfume.

'We shall have to take the long way round,' the cabman said, when he was settled back behind his steering-wheel. My eyes were agog. There were buttons and knobs on his control panel. There was a gauge that looked like a watch, embedded in the panelling. Sensational.

'I appreciate that,' said Mama. She appeared to be wholly recovered. Her eyes were red-rimmed but otherwise she was the woman I needed her to be.

'What I have in mind is straight up to Paddington,' said the cabbie, 'then Marylebone, Euston, then scoot back down to Bloomsbury.'

'Whatever you think,' sighed Mama, leaning her head back on the seat.

A couple of minutes later, the cabbie added, 'Where are you, exactly?'

There was no reply from Mama. She was breathing gently and regularly, her fleecy blonde hair hanging over her closed eyes.

'What street in Bloomsbury, madam?' the cabbie persisted, a little louder this time.

I cleared my throat, hoping it would wake Mama. Then I said, 'Calthorpe Street.'

'Right you are, sir,' said the cabbie. I had never been called 'sir' before. It made me prouder than I could have imagined. From now on I would hold my head high in Torrington Infants, come what may.

That's about as much as I have to tell, really. The remainder of that day is a blur. I think that on the long drive back to Bloomsbury, I may have conducted some sort of conversation with the driver, about three-cylinder engines or some such topic. Or maybe I'm imagining this. Suddenly 1908 seems a very long time ago, and of course it *is*. There are nurses working here who regard the moon landing as ancient history.

I suppose Mama and I got home all right. Yes, I'm sure we did. I can't remember any tearful reunion with Papa and Aunt Primrose. They were probably still in Hyde Park. Political speeches take a long time, longer than a child can conceive of. I suppose my mother and I had something to eat. Maybe we went straight to bed and had a nap. Really, I'm speculating here. I must have been terribly weary. As I am now, in fact.

Yes, it was an extraordinary day, a grand day. For me, as well as for the women of the western world. Of course, within a few years, World War One broke out, and all the suffragettes stopped asking for the vote and started campaigning against the Hun. They changed the name of their newspaper to *Britannia*, and Mrs Pankhurst said that anyone who wasn't pure English shouldn't be allowed to work for the government. My mother and Aunt Primrose would've found that most offensive, I'm sure, but thankfully we'd moved away from London by then, and my parents were too busy earning a living to spare much thought for speeches. Thankfully, too, I was too young to enlist, because I'm sure I would have, just to prove I wasn't a mummy's boy, and then what would've happened? I'd have found out that human beings are bags of soup just as my Mama said, and that the right kind of injury can spill them all over the ground.

But forgive me: I'm worn out, and the nurses are looking worried. Yes, they are! I have an eye for these things, doddery as I am. That girl over there, now, she's my favourite. We talk nineteen to the dozen while she's sprucing me up in the mornings; I swear I know more about her than her boyfriends do. Oh, but she's lovely, a little treasure. And such a soft touch; such soft hands! No, no, I can see what you're thinking. You *will* read sex into everything, won't you? Please remember that I'm from a bygone era; sex hadn't even been invented then. Why, if I'd been born just one day earlier, I'd have been a Victorian, wouldn't I? And you know what those Victorians were like.

But seriously, dear: I'm exhausted. All I've done is reminisce, and yet I've never felt so tired; as soon as these little angels put me to bed I'll be out like a light. But tomorrow is another day! Come back tomorrow, and I will tell you the rest. Everything you still want to know, I promise. Tomorrow.